Long Stories Short

A collection of short stories

Karen Black

Published by Karen Black

ISBN: 1497396085
ISBN-13: 978-1497396081

April 2014

Credits

Editors, Robert L. Arend and Joyce A. Carran

Cover Design: Dark Water Arts Design
Candace Bowser, Graphic Artist

KINDLE EDITON

Table of Contents

Dedication

This book is dedicated to my best friend, my husband, Rick Burd. His support and encouragement make life magical and keep it full of everyday miracles.

The Hunted

Flowing clouds shaded the full moon, briefly changing the otherwise well-lit landscape into a comforting and dark woodland. Shadows melted into the trees and created hiding places in every direction. Hiding places were necessary. A cool breeze stirred the branches, rustling the leaves and the undergrowth and disguising the sound of her steps as she crept through the forest.

As the moon peeked out from its temporary cover, Yvonne veered toward a group of sycamore trees lining the base of an upgrade. With her heart pounding and her breath coming in short, ragged bursts, she leaned against the rough trunk of one of the larger trees. As she tried to melt into the bark, she imagined the old tree could wrap its branches around her and keep her safely invisible to passersby. Standing motionless, she took long, deep breaths while she waited for the clouds to dim the moon and allow the cover of darkness to mask her movements again.

The sharp crack of a breaking branch pierced the silence, and she smelled his now familiar odor. The scent of sweat and stale beer told her he was close. Thankful for the overcast sky, Yvonne prayed the clouds would keep the moon shielded until he moved on. Her gaze darted in every direction until she found him. An imposing presence, his broad, square shoulders supported bulging biceps and sculpted forearms. A canvas vest covered his upper body and a quiver of arrows was slung across his back. Dark brown waves of hair skimmed his shoulders and covered much of his face. A long, thick knife hung from a leather belt around his waist. He carried a bow in his left hand.

Yvonne held her breath. The hunter stopped just ten feet from the old sycamore tree, where she pressed her body tightly against the trunk. A raccoon darted across the trail. The sound of the scampering creature drew the hunter's attention. He pulled an arrow from his quiver as he looked toward it. When he saw it was not her, he replaced the arrow, turned, and strode back in the direction from which he had come. When he was out of sight, Yvonne inched her body to the opposite side of the tree and continued her journey in an effort to travel as far from the hunter as she could. Lost in the wilderness, she knew there must be a road or a game trail somewhere that would lead her to safety.

For the first few minutes after she saw him, Yvonne moved cautiously to avoid stepping on brittle branches or crisp vegetation. When she was confident, the hunter had gone far enough away so that her steps would not be heard, she began to run. With a long, smooth stride, she traveled like a marathon runner, breathing deeply and evenly as she moved through the forest. When she thought she heard the distant rumble of an engine, she increased her speed. Maybe a road was closer than she realized. As the clouds dissipated, a game trail through the forest became visible, but so did she.

Yvonne sensed the arrow before a sharp pain exploded along the side of her neck. Now racing as fast as her legs would carry her, she felt the warmth from the blood trickling from the gash in her neck, across her collarbone, and down her chest. If the arrow had struck an inch to the right, she would be dying. The projectile would have gone straight through her throat. But it wasn't an inch to the right, and she wasn't dying. Yvonne was alive and determined to stay that way. She had to outrun him, and she would. Pain and fear urged her on.

Feet pounding in rhythm with her heart, her breath coming in gasps, Yvonne kept running, but her legs were losing strength. Afraid she couldn't go much farther, to stop meant to die, so she fought to keep moving. The pounding of the hunter's footsteps behind her told her he was gaining ground. For a few seconds, her eyes left the trail, as she glanced back over her shoulder, then stepped into the trap. As the rope noose tightened around her ankle and lifted her into the air, she gasped before an involuntary shriek escaped from her mouth.

***

Her scream blended into the sound of a coyote howling in the distance and startled Yvonne awake. Her head ached slightly and her neck was stiff. Maybe she'd feel better after she got up and moved around. She rolled out of bed and stumbled across the plush, ivory-colored carpet. Bleary-eyed, she lifted the blinds and opened the window. The sun, low in the burnished orange sky, peeked over the horizon. A hint of sunrays danced across the field of lavender, and the fragrance filled the room. With the promise of a clear, bright morning, Yvonne breathed in the lavender's relaxing scent as it drifted from her garden through the open window. The fragrance coaxed her to hurry outside and tend to the herbs.

She glanced back at the bed and smiled at Elektra, the long-haired little gray cat who was curled up on top of it. The cat raised her head in disgust, as if to say it was much too early for anything to disrupt her slumber, then closed her eyes and snuggled down into the depths of the comfortable bed clothes. With a deep breath and a heavy sigh, Yvonne looked longingly at the king-sized bed and the plush blankets. They seemed to invite her to slide once more under the mint-colored comforter.

Elektra had no trouble sleeping, except on those occasions the cat was disturbed by Yvonne's tossing and turning, mumbling, or screaming as though being chased, or even caught by the hounds of hell. She was happy the cat had adjusted to the disruptions rather than deciding to sleep elsewhere. Yvonne wondered if the little feline thought that, by staying close, she was protecting Yvonne from the monsters that invaded her psyche. Whatever the reason, Yvonne found it comforting to have Elektra close by.

Her life would be perfect if only she could sleep, but she couldn't shake the nightmares. Yesterday, someone came to her looking for help with an injury on his forearm. Yvonne had given him Devil's Claw when Horsetail would have been the better remedy. While the Devil's Claw would do no harm and would be of some help, it was a mistake that she would not have made if she had not been exhausted.

I wish sometimes that I could be a cat, Yvonne thought. *Maybe then I could sleep in peace.*

Yvonne worked every day in her garden. Her livelihood came from the herbal plants and the vegetables which grew plentifully under her careful watch. She provided not only for herself but for others in the area and some who were just passing through. Her garden was well known and often sought. Taught by her mother and grandmother, as they had been taught by generations before them, Yvonne had vast knowledge of plants' properties, medicinal as well as nutritional. She loved her garden. One day, she hoped to have a daughter who would absorb the lessons and carry on the family's traditions.

She spent the day tending to her patrons and the visitors who stopped to see her. She gathered herbs, tied them in bundles, then removed the ripe vegetables, and piled them under the trees in the shade. Sometimes entire families visited her garden, but more often it was one individual at a time. She enjoyed being able to interact with so many. Her customers came back repeatedly and told their friends about her garden. As a result, her clientele continued to expand. While many were repeat visitors, she welcomed a number of travelers that she would never meet again.

Sitting by the edge of the pond, she tried again to understand why her dreams had turned to nightmares. She had always dreamed, but in the last few weeks, her nighttime visions were terrifying and made her afraid of sleep. When exhaustion forced her to surrender to slumber, she was immersed in a dreamscape of hunters chasing her down and determined to kill her. Terror would force her awake, unrested and tense.

Last night, she had dreamed of being hit with an arrow and lifted in a catapult trap. She'd snapped awake, her muscles stiff and sore and her neck aching. Her throat was even a little raw. She suspected it was her own scream that woke her, not the coyote's mournful song. Her dreams were invading her life.

When day turned to dusk, Yvonne walked back to her home, where dinner and her little gray companion would give her some comfort before she fell into what she expected would be another troubled sleep.

***

When Yvonne awakened, she was confused. She remembered being chased by the hunter and then hoisted into the air. She thought she might have screamed before everything had gone black. After squinting her eyes open long enough to realize she was lying on the ground inside what appeared to be a cave, she closed them again. Not sure if she was alone, she kept still and listened, pretending to be asleep.

A few seconds later, someone began tapping her shoulder, shaking her arm, and shoving her gently. Still, she kept her eyes closed, trying to figure out how she had gotten to the dark, damp cavern.

"Wake up," a deep voice whispered. "Come on, girl. We need to get out of here before morning."

Yvonne opened her eyes and turned her head toward the voice. A large knee was situated next to her arm. She lifted her gaze past the knee and above a broad chest, to the face of the voice that had spoken to her. Dark raisin-colored eyes looked intently into hers.

"I'm Armond," he said in response to her confused expression. "The hunter had his arm around your neck. You passed out. He was cutting the rope to drop you to the ground when I hit him."

"I'm Yvonne," she said.

Armond continued, "I hit him hard enough to keep him from getting up, then I brought you here. For now, there is one less to hunt us, but we need to move away from this place in case he wakes. When the others discover him, awake or not, they will search thoroughly and could find this cave."

"Thank you," she murmured, lifting herself up with her elbows.

Armond nodded. "Now we need to travel, Yvonne. I know a

place where we can rest. It's on the other side of the field, past the rocks. We need to go now and we must hurry. It is getting close to dawn and we cannot cross the field in the daylight without being seen. When I saw them last, the hunters were behind us below the ridge."

"A hunter has been following me for days," she said. "And there are others nearby."

He offered her a small sack of dried fruit and nuts. "Eat."

When the scent of dried berries reached her nose, Yvonne's mouth filled with saliva. She hadn't realized how hungry she was and gratefully took the food from him.

"Come," he said when she'd eaten. "We must go now."

With Armond in the lead, they left the cave. His long stride covered a lot of ground and the strength in his muscular thighs was apparent as he moved quickly, yet effortlessly. Yvonne made sure she didn't drop too far back, sometimes breaking into a jog to stay close to him as they navigated the rough terrain under the night sky.

When darkness gave way to dawn, the sun rose over the mountains, promising a bright morning, which would stop their travel. As daylight crept over them, Armond slowed his pace.

"There's a rock overhang just beyond the river," he told her. "The overhang camouflages the narrow entrance to a cave. We'll be able to rest there. Others are waiting. They have food and will protect us while we sleep. But we need to get through that field. Can you travel quickly for a few more miles?"

"Lead the way," Yvonne panted. "I'll be close behind you."

Armond began to run, and Yvonne dashed after him. They were three quarters of the way across the field when an arrow came from the left. It passed Yvonne's cheek and stopped when it struck Armond's ribs. He took two steps, then fell to the ground.

Yvonne dropped to her knees beside him. The arrow had deeply pierced his side. His eyes reflected pain as he struggled to his feet. "Keep running until you find a place to hide," he panted. "When darkness falls, go to the cave as soon as you can. Take this." He held out a knife with a strip of rawhide wrapped around it. "Now, go."

Yvonne took the handmade weapon from Armond and ran toward the river. Her lungs were burning. Her mouth was dry. Tears blurred her vision as they poured down her cheeks. She heard the hunters behind her. Somehow, she found another gear and increased her distance from them. She saw the rock overhang at the edge of the field ahead. It was exactly as Armond had described but knew she couldn't reach the cave without being seen.

As the sun crept up over the horizon, it reflected off the river's surface. In minutes, it would be full daylight. She needed a place to hide. As if in answer to a silent plea, the river made a sharp curve to the right, where trees lining the bank briefly hid her from the pursuing hunters.

If the trees block their view long enough, she thought, *I can disappear.*

There was only one place to hide. She looked up at the trees. Yvonne focused on the sturdy but low-hanging branches of a huge old maple tree. Without another thought, she climbed up the branches like a staircase into the thick leaves, and prayed the hunters would not look up.

***

When Yvonne awoke, Elektra was rubbing against her cheek. The cat's soft whiskers tickled her nose. Yvonne yawned and got stiffly out of bed to make a breakfast of eggs and vegetables. She finished eating quickly and went out to get her garden in order. She expected many visitors, since the cold weather would soon be approaching.

Most days Elektra stayed inside until afternoon, but today the cat joined Yvonne and sat beside her at the edge of the pond. The ducks were splashing and swimming and diving into the pond for minnows, but Elektra didn't seem interested in them. She curled up on Yvonne's lap, purring contentedly. It was mid-morning when a family arrived looking for vegetables.

Yvonne helped them gather what they needed. The visitors talked for a while and then continued down the road. They were not from the area, but just passing through. Friends had told them about Yvonne's garden, they told her, so they made a detour to stop and visit. She loved her job.

The day passed quickly until sunset, when pink and red colors slashed the blue sky. Yvonne was tired. She had fought to stay awake all day. It would have been so easy to nap in the afternoon, but she had fought the urge to sleep and continued to fight it. If she could stay awake for a few more hours, she would be worn out by nightfall. Maybe then she would be too tired to dream.

***

After the hunters passed below her, Yvonne wedged herself firmly within the thick branches of the fifty-foot-tall tree. Straddling one broad branch, she wrapped her arms around the smaller branches. Though she rarely stayed in one place for long, grabbing sleep wherever she could find shelter, Yvonne fell asleep hugging the tree and slept through the day.

It was dusk when she opened her eyes. The huge soft leaves of the tree brushed against her face. The only sound was the rushing of the river. Still, she remained motionless. Until she could review her current circumstances and location, caution remained her first priority.

Turning her head slowly, she scanned the area below and saw no sign of the hunters. The sun hung low in the sky and would soon be out of sight. The leaves of the tree protected her from the wind, which began to increase. She had to cross the rest of the field to get to the shelter Armond had described. The rock overhang did a good job of disguising the entrance to the cave, and she hoped the hunters had not discovered it.

Yvonne stood on the branch and stretched to chase the stiffness from her muscles. She checked to be sure she still had Armond's knife. It remained fastened to the strap she'd wrapped around her wrist. She ran her fingers over the knife's grip, then climbed down to the bottom of the tree. After slowly making her way to the river, she drank from the fast moving, icy water. She quenched her thirst, then moved away from the bank. Staying within an arm's reach of the trees, she crept through the field toward the rocks.

The weight surprised her when it dropped onto Yvonne's back. The pressure knocked her to the ground with a thud and took her breath away.

The arrow has found me, she thought. In a panic, she tried to scramble to her feet but felt the smooth, heavy mass move to her shoulder—not an arrow—it was a snake. Her body reacted at the same time her brain processed the attack. The giant constrictor had dropped from the tree and was wrapping itself around her.

Thankful her arms were free, she grabbed Armond's knife and slashed at the creature. Blood ran down her chest, but rather than release her, the snake squeezed her tighter. With newfound strength, she stabbed the reptile again and kept cutting until the weight slid away from her shoulder. The beast kept squeezing her chest, but she was winning the battle and felt the pressure diminish. Still, she had difficulty getting a full breath, and she knew there wasn't much time left before the animal repositioned itself. The snake had slithered its giant body lower and used its tail to pin her arms to her sides.

Barely able to move her forearms, Yvonne pointed the knife upward and sliced her captor's underside. This time, when the snake released its grip, it dropped to the ground, writhing for several seconds before it stilled.

Shaking from the amount of adrenaline she had needed to battle her attacker, she detoured to the river flowing nearby. The cold water would help ease the burning she felt in her arms and would also wash off the blood and entrails that covered her.

Despite the time lost fighting the snake and discomfort resulting from the attack, Yvonne was grateful for the food the snake's carcass would provide. She planned to carry a part of it as she traveled the last leg of her journey. In exchange for the shelter, she could share the meat with the others at the cave.

Her euphoria dimmed when she got to the river and realized that some of the blood covering her chest was her own. In her struggle with the boa, she had cut through the snake and into her upper arm. When she cleaned the blood, she saw a deep gash on her left arm and shoulder. She put pressure on the wounds, which were bleeding profusely. Coupled with the cool water of the river, the pressure stopped the bleeding. Yvonne knew, however, that any stress would start the blood flowing again. That meant carrying a substantial piece of snake meat was out of the question.

Nothing more I can do now, she thought. *I need to get to the cave. Armond said I can rest there and find help.* She ate a few bites of the raw meat, then draped a small part of the tail behind her neck and down over her uninjured shoulder. She walked toward the rocks.

Even moving more slowly than she would have preferred, Yvonne's energy quickly drained. The cliffs were farther away than they appeared. Her shoulder ached and the shifting weight of the snake caused it to bleed again. One foot in front of the other, she kept the rock overhang in sight and moved steadily toward it.

***

When Yvonne felt a gentle tapping on her cheek, she moaned, "Go back to sleep, Elektra." The tapping continued until she opened her eyes and saw the familiar window of her bedroom. Daylight found its way through the glass, but the sky was overcast and she smiled at the thought of rain. She loved the rain, and it would be good for the garden.

She reached for Elektra and buried her fingers in the cat's soft fur. When she closed her eyes, the tapping began again. Elektra was doing everything she could to keep her from drifting back to sleep, but Yvonne was comfortable and content.

***

"Wake up. Open your eyes."

"Elektra?" Yvonne murmured, her fingers still entwined in the cat's fur. When she opened her eyes, the eyes gazing back at hers were not those of Elektra. They were the dark eyes of a woman who, although older, looked very much like Yvonne.

As Yvonne sat up, she released her grip on the fur-covered skin beneath her. She was dizzy. How could the room be spinning? She fell back onto the bed. But the bed wasn't her soft mattress. There was no scent of lavender, nor were there pastel-colored walls. Instead, she saw straw. She was lying on the rocky, straw-covered floor of a high-ceilinged cave.

The woman stroked her arm and said, "You've been sick for days, but you'll be fine. We found you at the edge of the field. You were lying at the foot of the rocks, holding a dead snake and delirious with fever."

Confused, Yvonne looked from the woman to the walls of the cavern and thought she must be a dreaming. As she closed her eyes, she remembered the snake. She remembered dreaming she'd awakened in a tree with the leaves brushing against her face when it had been Elektra's paw rubbing her cheek. Elektra had been trying to wake her then, the same way she was trying to wake her now.

Stroking Yvonne's arm, the woman said, "My name is Hannah."

Squeezing her eyes shut, Yvonne muttered, "This is all a dream. It's a nightmare. I've been so tired, and Elektra kept trying to wake me. I wanted to sleep, but now I want to wake up."

"It has been a nightmare for all the forest people since the hunters came this time," Hannah told her. "We heard about a young female who had been chased from their camp and we thought they had taken you. You crossed the road and wandered too far, but you will be safe now. Few hunters come over to this side of the forest and we have many places to hide from them."

"Yvonne," a voice whispered.

At the sound of the familiar voice, Yvonne opened her eyes. "Armond," she stammered as she sat up and looked for him. A smile erupted when her gaze settled on Armond, who stood looking down at her.

"You are here!" she gasped. "After you were shot, I didn't see you. I thought they had killed you."

"They thought so, too," he said. "I waited until they passed, then I backtracked and hid in the trees by the river. I was sick for days and lost track of you."

Everything came flooding back into her mind. She had seen pictures of pastel-colored rooms in magazines that the campers sometimes left. Pictures were treasures. When campers were close, she often hovered outside their tents, eavesdropping and watching.

She had been sitting near a campsite when the hunters saw her. They startled her and she ran in fear, not looking for the paths she knew. They chased her and she ran across the road toward the river. There were so many hunters. The chase separated her from the rest of the clan. For weeks, she had been trying to find her way back.

In terror and exhaustion, Yvonne had confused her dreams with reality. She didn't have a garden to tend. Her gardens were in the fields within the forests, where she foraged for herbs and vegetation and shared her bounty with the others. She didn't have a pet cat. Her four-legged companions were the feral creatures who roamed the countryside. She didn't have a bedroom with a bed and plush blankets. Her mattress was made of ferns and straw; her bedroom was a corner of one of the many caves within the mountains where she traveled with the clan. Yvonne remembered it all now. She had been hunted for her entire life.

The hunters thought she was an animal, but she wasn't. She was what the hunters shouted when they saw her—a "Sasquatch."

###

Aftermath

"Ronnie, wake up."

"It's the middle of the night," Ronnie mumbled.

"Wake up, Veronica. Get Michelle. We need to go," Paul said sternly.

"Paul? What? What time is it?"

Ronnie glanced at the clock on her nightstand. It was 3:00 a.m. She put the pillow over her head.

"You need to get up, Veronica. Now! There's a fire."

She heard the crackling. The room was too bright. Turning toward the light, Ronnie realized there were flames where the closet door was supposed to be. She was instantly wide awake and hollered to her sister, who was sleeping in the bedroom down the hall, "Michelle, Michelle, wake up!"

The flames were bright enough to light the room. They were dropping down the closet door from the ceiling, rather than climbing up from the floor, indicating that the fire started above her.

Paul was standing at the bedroom door. "The door is cool. It's safe to go into the hall," he told her. "We need to wake Michelle and get outside quickly. The roof is burning."

"Michelle! Michelle? Wake up!" Ronnie called again, as she moved through the bedroom door into the hall, turning right toward Michelle's bedroom. She reached Michelle's room in three long strides. Just as Ronnie touched the doorknob, the door opened and her sister dashed toward her.

"I smelled smoke," Michelle said. There was panic in her eyes.

Paul went to the top of the staircase to see if it was safe to go down.

Ronnie grabbed Michelle's hand and, moving toward the stairs, told her, "The house is on fire. It must have started on the roof, or maybe in the attic. There are flames in my room, but nothing in the hall, and the staircase is clear. We will be able to get out if we move quickly. Come on." Ronnie had every confidence that Paul would lead them to safety. After all, he was a fireman.

"Stay behind me," Paul said.

Michelle allowed Ronnie to pull her along the hallway to the staircase that would take them to the first floor of the duplex. They were almost at the bottom of the stairs when they heard a loud crack. Paul stopped, bringing Ronnie to a halt right behind him. A smoking ceiling beam fell directly in front of them, allowing them a glimpse of the flaming attic above.

If Paul hadn't stopped, Ronnie thought, *I would be under that beam, not behind it.*

Paul stepped over the beam and said, "The fire is burning fast. This old house isn't going to last much longer." He continued to move down the staircase. Ronnie stepped over the smoldering wood. Michelle followed her. Everybody was coughing.

"What about Alice and Donna?" Michelle asked, tears in her eyes. Alice and Donna lived in the other half of the duplex and were like family to Ronnie and Michelle.

"Grab the cell phone on the table by the door," Ronnie told Michelle. "We'll call them as soon as we get outside."

The ceiling beam was smoldering on the staircase, but the flames had not yet ignited the first floor. Michelle grabbed the cell phone from the table.

When they reached the front door, Paul took one last look at the staircase before he followed the two women out the door to safety.

Michelle dialed Alice's number as she stepped out onto the porch, sirens in the distance, letting her know fire trucks were on the way. When Alice's phone continued to ring, Michelle said a silent prayer that Alice and Donna were already out. Maybe they had called 911.

Suddenly, there was a loud cracking noise and the west corner of the duplex collapsed. It was the side where Alice's and Donna's bedrooms were located. Michelle froze.

Ronnie shouted, "Get off the porch, Michelle. Move out into the yard." She turned back toward the house to help her sister. At the same time Ronnie's foot hit the first step, Paul hollered, "Ronnie, look out!" She turned toward Paul, who was reaching for her, when the porch roof collapsed on top of her. Paul grabbed for her as the last of the wood fell. There was nothing he could do but scream, "Veronica!"

Michelle dropped the phone and turned toward the rubble. She felt something hit her head, and everything went black.

***

"Wow!" Alice turned, tears in her eyes, and said to Donna, "I can't believe the fire moved through the house so quickly. I thought we were going to die. It was terrifying." She stood staring at what was left of the house.

The newspaper was on the ground, soggy and ripped, but with the headline still visible:

Two Dead in House Fire

"It won't be the same without Ronnie and Michelle," Donna sobbed. "Even if we could rebuild the house, I don't want to do it. I'll miss them too much. The house will be a constant reminder that we lost them."

"It is so sad to see our house like this. I loved the old place," Alice told Donna as they walked across the dark yard toward the front porch of the burned house. Both women ducked under the yellow police tape.

"This is where the roof collapsed. It was right at the top of the stairs where they fell," Alice said. "It's almost as if I remember seeing it happen."

"Donna? Do you think we can contact them?" Alice whispered to her friend, her grief giving way to wonder.

"If we can contact anyone, it will be Ronnie. She was always studying the paranormal. She believed in life after death. You know the premonitions she had. Nine times out of ten, they were right on," Donna said. "I think we should try to talk to her. If there's a way to respond, Ronnie will find it."

"Let's do a séance. When Ronnie did the séances, she lit candles and simply talked to the spirits," Donna told her. "Remember how she could almost always find a spirit to respond? If she knows we're trying to contact her, I just know she'll answer."

Alice slowly covered the ground to the porch. It was strange to feel as if she was trespassing on her own property, but the whole situation seemed strange. She walked up to the steps and said, "I think if we try to reach her, it should be right here, where she left us."

Alice dropped to the ground and sat cross-legged, and Donna sat in front of her.

"Take my hands," Donna told Alice. They joined hands and closed their eyes.

"Veronica Palmer, please come to us. Veronica Palmer, we invite you to join us this evening. If you can hear me, please acknowledge our invitation," Alice said.

Nothing happened.

"Donna." Alice turned to her friend. "You try."

Donna took a deep breath and whispered, "Veronica Palmer, Ronnie, are you there? Ronnie, talk to us."

The night remained silent. The moon was just a sliver in the sky, and it seemed like there were a billion stars. It was clear, and though not bright, there was enough light to see the details of their surroundings.

"Do you think it's too soon after she died?" Donna asked.

"No. I think we just need to be patient," Alice replied. "She's new at being on the other side, and it might take a little time."

"Did you feel that?" Alice asked. "I felt a cold wind."

"I felt it, but I think it was just an evening breeze," Donna told her.

"Ronnie, is that you? Can you talk to us?" Alice asked excitedly.

"Ronnie, where are you? Are you here with us?" Donna called.

"I think you should only ask one question at a time," Alice said.

Donna continued, "Ronnie, can you give us some kind of sign that you're here?"

A stone rolled about three inches, moving toward Alice's knee. Alice and Donna locked eyes and said simultaneously, "She's here."

"Maybe she's tired," Donna suggested. "It probably takes an awful lot of energy to communicate between worlds."

"You might be right," Alice said. "Remember when she first started talking to Paul, after he died last year? Initially, it was just a dream or two. After a couple of months, she said she could hear his voice in her head. Lately, she talked about him like he was still alive. She said their link became stronger, and he had decided to stay with her. She was excited about it."

"I wonder if she was really communicating with him, or if she was imagining what he would say to her?" Donna asked.

"She always was a bit psychic. After Paul died, she became more intent on learning all she could about psychic connections," Alice replied.

It was then that Donna and Alice saw the man approaching them. "Alice," Donna whispered, "I think we're in trouble. There's a police officer coming. We shouldn't be inside the police tape."

"It's okay, Donna. After all, it's our house," Alice told her. "Anyway, it's a fireman. See the uniform?"

The man continued toward Donna and Alice. He stopped at the yellow tape and said, "Hello, Alice, Donna."

It was Alice who recognized him first. "Paul?" she stuttered, "Oh, my heavens! Paul! We can see you. Ronnie really did see you and she talked to you. I wasn't sure. Is she with you now?"

Paul replied, "Ronnie can't leave Michelle. Ronnie is going to be fine. Except for some burns on her arm and a broken shoulder, she came through in good shape. Michelle, however, is in a coma. Ronnie has been talking to her and is coaxing her back, but she heard you calling her. She asked me to come to you and explain."

Alice was the first to speak. "What are you saying? Are Ronnie and Michelle alive? But we saw the newspaper. We saw the headline. Two people died in that fire."

It was then that Donna understood. She ran to the newspaper and got on her knees to read the report below the headline. She gasped before calling back to Alice, "It wasn't Ronnie and Michelle who died in the fire. It was us!"

###

You Summoned Me

The intercom buzzed. Irritated at the intrusion, Mark punched the reply button and snapped, "What is it?"

"Sorry to bother you, Mark," his secretary replied. "Erin is on the line. She said it's important. Shall I put her through?"

"Thanks, Marion. I didn't mean to bark at you."

"No problem," Marion chuckled.

Despite the interruption, Mark grinned as he reached for the phone. Erin had that effect on him.

"Hey, what's up?"

"Is there any chance you'd be able to get out of the office early? I have an enormous surprise and if I need to wait until this evening, I'll explode."

Laughing, Mark replied, "That sounds intriguing. I can finish this project in about an hour. Will that work?"

"That will be perfect. You won't believe what I found," Erin said.

"I'll head for home as soon as I can." Mark hung up the phone. He shook his head and wondered what she had up her sleeve. Erin's frequent surprises were always entertaining.

Erin had spent the afternoon at the auction house, where she discovered an unexpected treasure. She'd won the bid for an antique Ouija board, carved from a solid chunk of hickory. The date, *March 15, 1891,* is etched on its reverse.

The Ides of March over one-hundred-twenty years ago, Erin thought. She believed the age of the board would make it a receptive and powerful tool. With rounded edges, the heart-shaped wooden planchette that accompanied the Ouija board had been well-used, and the hole in its center was perfectly round. Overall, the condition of her prize was remarkable. Excited about using the talking board later that night, Erin couldn't wait to show Mark.

***

"Ouija board?" Mark laughed. "You're kidding."

"Mark, it's an antique. Age makes it powerful."

"You truly believe this wooden tray will allow you to talk to dead people?"

"Yes," she retorted. "The Ouija board is a channeling device for contacting spirits. When someone touches the planchette, it concentrates that person's energy in one place. That energy gives the spirits an invitation to respond by guiding the planchette to spell words and answer questions.

Mark was unconvinced, but Erin's enthusiasm was contagious. "Okay, my mystical spouse. Get some candles. I'll grab the card table and meet you in the living room."

Mark set up the card table, and Erin placed the Ouija board on top of it. She lit three candles and turned off the lights.

"So, what do we do now?" Mark asked.

Erin said, "Put your fingers on the edge of the planchette and ask if any spirits are present. Then invite them to come."

"If any spirits are here, I invite you to join us," Mark said.

They waited silently, but when three minutes passed and nothing happened, Mark lifted his hands from the planchette.

"How long does it take for a spirit to answer us?" Mark asked.

Erin dropped her hands to her lap. "I don't know. A few minutes, I guess. Maybe there aren't any spirits listening."

And then the planchette shifted its position ever so slightly. With her moss-colored eyes wide open and her shoulders frozen in a shrugged position. Erin looked at Mark. His wrinkled forehead and raised eyebrows told her he'd seen it, too. Without speaking, the couple placed their fingertips on the edges of the wooden heart.

"This is a safe place for you to enter," Erin whispered. "You are welcome in our home."

Slowly, yet steadily, the planchette moved. It stopped on the letter C.

"Did you do that?"

"No," she stammered, sure that Mark hadn't guided their fingers across the board. "It was pulling my hands."

Fingers touching the planchette, Erin concentrated on the Ouija board and asked, "Do you have a message for us?"

Again, the planchette moved. It picked up speed with each letter it covered, as it slid from the C to the O, then the M and on to I N G N O W.

The flames from the candles flickered and one was extinguished as a mild breeze swept through the room. For a split second, the card table vibrated.

Erin pulled her fingers from the planchette, reached across the table, and clasped Mark's hand as an entity materialized at the far end of the room. They sat immobile and watched the ethereal form creep slowly toward them. Though small in stature, the dark entity had a presence that filled the room. Golden eyes glowed—like a fire had been lit within their center. The creature cocked its head slightly to the right, its piercing eyes seemed to stare through Mark.

What have we done?

Mark hesitated, then greeted the apparition, "Hello."

Erin slid from her chair and stood behind her husband.

As the entity grew, its misty form became an amber-colored pelt that covered the muscular body of a magnificent lioness. Her glowing eyes changed from gold to emerald, and her thick coat glistened in the candlelight.

With a soft growl, she said, "You summoned me."

Startled at the sound of its voice, Mark jumped backward in his chair. "I can hear you."

"You connected our spirits," the apparition chanted. "My thoughts become words, but I speak only to you."

"Leave now," Erin commanded. "You are not welcome here."

But the cat's attention was on Mark. As if Erin had not spoken, the lioness moved to Mark's side. Purring loudly, she rubbed her head against his shoulder. The soft fur on the tip of her ears brushed Mark's chin as the weight of the cat threw him off balance. He stood and his chair fell backward.

Erin dashed toward the door, but the lioness pounced, knocking her to the floor. Front feet on the woman's shoulders, the cat snarled, then licked Erin's cheek, its rough tongue scraping her skin.

As quickly as it pounced on top of her, the sleek beast turned back to Mark. The cat grabbed Mark's head with her front feet, sank her glistening teeth into his throat, and dissolved as Mark collapsed to the floor.

"Mark," Erin screamed.

She raced across the room, kneeled beside her husband, and tried without success to stop the blood gushing from his torn jugular.

Pressing her cheek against his, she sobbed, "I am so sorry." Through tear-filled eyes, she watched a translucent black panther spring from Mark's chest.

"You summoned me," were the last words Erin heard.

###

Magic or Miracles

The roar of the ocean was continuous. The water swelled with each incoming wave before collapsing on the sand, where the foamy liquid slid back to meet the next fluid peak and repeat the process. The endless waves were driven by a storm far out to sea, a storm invisible from land, even as the sun climbed and sparkled in the union of saltwater and beach sand.

Andy paced. Katie should have arrived half an hour ago. He tried to compose himself with a notion of Katie having difficulty hailing a cab, but the boat was packed and he was ready to ride the waves. The weatherman had predicted clear skies, low humidity, and winds of three to five knots.

Then he spotted her.

"A perfect day for boating," Katie hollered from the end of the dock, her dazzling smile clearly visible. The breeze caught her shoulder length hair, swirling it around the light complexion of her face like an auburn halo.

Andy's eyes lingered over his wife as she strolled gracefully toward him. "Every day is perfect," Andy replied with a wry smile. "Weather permitting," he added.

"What kept you?" He asked, "Trouble getting away from the station?" Katie had an early morning radio show and was typically at the studio until about 8:00 a.m.

Her emerald-green eyes bright with anticipation, she looked up at him and whispered, "I got out a little early, but there was a major traffic jam, and I was stuck in the middle of it. I called you and left a message. I asked you not to leave without me." She chuckled, knowing there was absolutely no way Andy would have gotten on that boat without her.

Reaching into his pocket, Andy realized his phone was still in the car. He sheepishly admitted, “I forgot it again.”

Katie laughed and rolled her eyes. “You need to put it on a chain and wear it around your neck.”

Andy unhitched the boat from the mooring and started the engine, slowly easing the craft away from the dock and out to the ocean. The boat moved away from the land and into the open water. As the boat picked up speed, the beach seemed to shrink until swallowed by the ocean.

While Katie lounged on the deck, reveling in the sun’s warmth, Andy piloted the boat with no specific destination in mind, his face bathed in mist and the warm sea breeze. Each was lost in thought, both enjoying the freedom from responsibility that their ocean voyages always provided.

After an hour or so, Katie moved next to Andy and said, “This looks like a good spot to find fish.”

“I’m trusting your judgment,” Andy said. “Ready to find some fish?”

“I’d love a swordfish dinner,” Katie replied. “Meanwhile, I’m going to take a nap and soak up more sun.” She stretched out again on the lounge chair.

The time seemed to pass quickly. Morning morphed to afternoon. Neither noticed the waves had intensified until the darkening sky replaced the warmth of the sun with the chill of an escalating breeze.

Katie opened her eyes. “The water is getting rough. The sky is getting darker, too.”

“I don’t think there’s a problem,” Andy told her. “It’s overcast, but the clouds are moving away quickly. There were no storms in the weather forecast.” They were about fifteen miles from the bay.

Katie said, “You’re probably right, but I’d feel better if we moved closer to shore. The weather might still turn wicked.”

Years with Katie had taught Andy to respect his wife's intuition. He gathered his fishing gear and prepared to turn the boat toward home.

The smoky clouds gradually turned to charcoal, shrouding the sun. The dark billows eliminated the ambient light. The wind amplified dangerously, whipping across the ocean surface as it gathered moisture and pelted the boaters with what felt like icy needles bouncing off their skin.

Andy hollered over his shoulder, "Is there any coffee left?"

When Katie didn't respond, he only assumed she had expected his request and already gone below into the cabin to make more coffee. He turned his attention back to the wheel.

A few minutes passed and Katie didn't return. Rain had begun to fall. Huge raindrops splattered down and splashed in the water covering the deck, left over from the waves that periodically washed its surface. The forecast had been wrong. A storm was chasing them.

Looking back across the boat, Andy was concerned that he didn't see his wife. Again, he called, "Katie? Where are you?"

Preparing to go below in search of her, it startled Andy when he realized she was standing right beside him, as though she popped out of nowhere. After twenty-seven years of marriage, Andy had never gotten used to that. It was as though he only had to think about Katie, and she would find him. If she was anywhere close, she would walk up to him; if she was away, she would call. It was almost eerie.

Shaking his head, Andy asked, "How do you do that?"

Katie shrugged her shoulders and responded with that familiar glint in her eye and a raised eyebrow, "It's magic." Smiling, she continued, "The wind doesn't seem as strong now. I think we've outrun the storm. Good thing because the radio isn't working."

"What's wrong with the radio?"

"It's dead. I can't even get any static." She said, "We

should probably call it a day."

Andy agreed. "I was thinking the same thing."

The trip back was not nearly as relaxing as the voyage earlier in the day. Though the wind had calmed somewhat, the waves were choppy and rose high enough to cause a jarring ride home. It was slow going, but they made it back without incident.

Arriving at the bay, Andy pulled the boat close to the dock, where he attached it to the mooring. The clouds had turned to a misty gray yet allowed some sunlight to filter through and glisten off the still wet deck. Various shades of pink illuminated the sky in the distance, promising a lovely day to follow.

Andy stowed the fishing gear, then boosted the cooler from the boat and onto the dock. Katie stepped from the boat and Andy followed, easily lifting the cooler that contained the day's catch to his shoulder, balanced with one arm. They walked the short distance to the parking lot, debating which wine would best complement their fish dinner.

At the car, Andy saw his telephone was on the front seat. He picked it up and checked for messages. Katie's number was there, along with the number of an unfamiliar caller who had tried to reach him three times.

"Mr. Donnelly, this is Melissa Cason, at Trinity Hospital," the unfamiliar woman's voice announced. "Please call me as soon as possible." Andy dialed the number she provided.

A receptionist answered, "Trinity Hospital."

"Hello, this is Andrew Donnelly. I have several messages to call this number and speak with Melissa Cason."

"I'll connect you," the woman replied.

"This is Melissa Cason," Andy recognized the voice as the one who had left the message.

"Hello, Ms. Cason. This is Andrew Donnelly. I had a message to contact you."

"Yes, thank you for calling. I am the RN in charge of the trauma unit. Everything is under control right now, but Katherine was in an accident. The EMTs brought her here, and the doctor has admitted her," Melissa told him.

"What happened? Is she badly hurt?"

"I'll go over the details when you get here," the nurse responded. "There is no need to rush. She is stable and comfortable. I'll be at the front desk, in the Trauma Unit, and will take you to her room as soon as you arrive."

Turning to his wife, Andy covered the phone with his hand and said hesitantly, "Kathy was in an accident. She's at Trinity."

He returned his attention to Nurse Cason and said, "We can be there in twenty minutes. Thank you."

When they arrived at the hospital, Katie whispered, "I'm going to the Chapel first. Go on ahead to the room. I'll see you in a few minutes."

Andy nodded, went to the desk and asked for directions to the Trauma Unit, where he met Melissa Cason. She was a stout woman, about the age of his mother, he thought. The nurse walked out from behind the desk, reached for Andy's hand, and said, "Mr. Donnelly, I'm so glad we could reach you."

"When did this happen? I'm sorry I was so late receiving your messages. We were out on the boat. I had forgotten my phone. Thank you for calling. My wife is in the Chapel. She will be right up." Andy realized he was rambling.

The RN was unruffled and reassuring as she placed her hand on his forearm and explained, "Katherine was in an automobile accident earlier in the day. She got to the emergency room at about 10:45 this morning. They transported her on a life flight. She has a broken shoulder, some spinal injury, and head trauma."

"Can I see her?" Andy interrupted.

"Of course," the nurse replied, "but Dr. Paulson wants to discuss her condition with you in the lounge. He'll meet you there shortly."

Andy repeated, "My wife is in the Chapel. Will someone

let her know to come to the lounge when she comes up?"

"Certainly," Nurse Cason replied.

Before they left the desk, a short, balding man, wearing a crisp white lab coat over pale green scrubs, approached. With sympathetic eyes and a mirthless smile, he extended his hand to Andy. "I'm Ron Paulson. Are you Mr. Donnelly?"

"Yes," Andy responded, shaking his hand.

"Please, come with me," the doctor said, then led Andy and the RN to the lounge around the corner. Andy sat on the vinyl sofa. The doctor sat in the chair next to him, took a deep breath, exhaled, then leaned close to Kathy's father. "Katherine was trapped in the vehicle for some time before the rescue unit could free her. When they got her out of the car, she wasn't breathing. The medics were able to revive her, but we have no way of knowing exactly how long she was without oxygen. It could have been seconds, or it could have been minutes."

His eyes were sympathetic, but his lips were taut. "There's something that I need you to understand. In most cases, the human brain can remain undamaged for up to six minutes without oxygen, but beyond that, there is almost always some damage. Usually, the next critical point is about ten minutes. If the brain does not have oxygen for ten minutes or more, it is highly likely that there will be significant neurological damage, and that cognitive function will be impaired to some extent. Of course, this varies from person to person. I must stress again that, although what I am telling you is typical, there are always exceptions. The third critical point is usually the fifteen-minute mark. At that point, it is almost impossible to restore cerebral function."

"But they revived her," Andy stammered, "so she's okay now. You said she was stable."

"Yes," Dr. Paulson continued. "She is stable, and that is important, but the concern right now is what will happen when she awakens. We must also be prepared for the possibility that she will not awaken. Katherine is in a coma. A coma is the body's way of protecting it and is not necessarily a bad thing after brain trauma. However, we will not have a reliable prognosis until she wakes up, and that is the other dilemma. A coma is unpredictable. It can last days, weeks, or even years."

"Kathy," he whispered, thinking back to the day his beautiful daughter had been born. It was twenty-four years ago, but he remembered every detail. The memory could have been no clearer had the birth occurred that same day. As a newborn, Kathy was a perfect little person, with the bluest of blue eyes, and tiny rose-colored lips he swore had smiled at him the day she was born. She was the image of her mother, in every respect but one: Katie was only five feet and two inches tall; but Kathy had reached a height of five feet and seven inches. Katie and Kathy, the two loves of his life.

"Can I see her now?" Andy asked the doctor. "My wife is in the Chapel, but she'll be here in a few minutes, I'm sure. I would appreciate it if you would let me explain the situation to her. She'll handle it better coming from me."

The doctor nodded. "Of course, I understand completely. Melissa, would you wait for Mrs. Donnelly while I escort Mr. Donnelly to Katherine's room?"

Traveling down the hall felt like a slow-motion walk to the gallows. Andy couldn't imagine losing his daughter, nor could he imagine her losing the ability to function normally. Ironically, Kathy was working on her doctorate in psychology. The workings of the mind had always fascinated her.

They entered her room, and the doctor asked, "Is there anything I can do for you?"

Andy shook his head and said, "Nothing except your best to repair any damage that has been done."

Dr. Paulson said, "That I will do. I'll leave you alone now. Stay for as long as you like and talk to her. I believe coma patients hear and understand conversation. It helps them focus, and I also believe it can encourage them to come back to us."

Andy looked around the dimly lit room before approaching the bed. He was not surprised by the equipment, the IV drips, the beeps and the flashing lights of the monitors. Kathy lay in the single hospital bed near the window of the private room. Her hair was hidden beneath a mound of bandages wrapped around her head like a helmet. Thick compresses covered her shoulder, with bandages hiding her upper arm, and a brace that kept her elbow in a 90-degree position across her chest. Her beautiful skin had turned into a horrifying combination of red, blue, and yellow. Stitches meandered from beneath her left eye, across her cheek and ended at her nose, then angled sharply down, ending at her lips. Abundant gauze was taped under her chin.

Taking a deep breath, Andy refused to give in to the tears that tried to escape. In his mind, he felt tears would be an admission he had lost his daughter. He needed to believe that she would recover unscathed.

Crossing the small room to Katherine's bedside, Andy forced a smile.

"The doctor said you were banged up pretty badly, but with a few weeks' rest, you'll be good as new."

Andy pulled the chair next to the bed and sat down. He thought how small his daughter looked, lying swaddled in sheets, gauze and cotton. When Andy lifted her hand, the sight of her fingers immediately bewildered him. They didn't belong to Katherine, but to Katie. He could see the ladder-shaped scar that stretched across the back of Katie's thumb, the result of an accident when his wife had been a child.

He knew, of course, what he was seeing wasn't possible, that stress can cause the mind to imagine strange things. He closed his eyes and willed his brain to clear and his body to relax. Yet, when he looked again, the pale hand was still covered by his palm. His daughter's larger, stronger hands could not have vanished within his grasp. And then he realized what caused the confusion. Katie and Kathy were both short for Katherine, and both women had the same last name.

Still trying to process what he was seeing, Andy thought about what had happened since that morning. He had seen Katie. They had carried on a conversation, but he couldn't remember if he had actually touched her. Had he imagined her presence? Had she been lying in that hospital bed alone while he was out playing in the ocean?

Andy reached for his telephone and scrolled to see if there was truly a message from his wife. It was there. He pressed the button for voice mail and listened. With sirens in the distance and voices in the background, he heard Katie's familiar voice, "*Hi Captain. This is your first mate. There was an accident. Traffic is stopped everywhere. There are fire trucks, ambulances, and even a helicopter hovering. I am right in the middle of the melee in the Taxi, and I think it's pretty bad. It looks like I'm going to be stuck here for a while. I don't want to ruin our plans, but I'm not sure if I can get to you this morning. If you don't see me shortly, you'll get another phone call. I love you.*" He checked the time of the call. It was 9:20 a.m.

Confused, he looked at Katie and stammered, "How did you do that?"

"Are you all right, Mr. Donnelly?"

Nurse Cason stood in the doorway, holding a blue bag.

"Please, tell me what happened to her," Andy pleaded, collapsing into a chair and crying.

"As I understand it, a truck lost its brakes at the top of Vine Street. You know how steep that hill is. It apparently gained momentum, so that it was traveling at a pretty high rate when it rammed the Taxi. The medic told me that the impact pushed the back door of the cab into the center of the vehicle. Somehow, Mrs. Donnelly was thrown sideways and pinned between the doors. We believe the seatbelt broke her shoulder when the backseat was pushed into a vertical position. Her head must have hit the door frame, which would have caused her skull injury."

The nurse stopped, then said in a rush, "Don't you give up hope. I've seen a lot of miracles in my time here. She could wake up at any moment and be right as rain. You just keep believing and keep talking to her. Let her know you want her to come back."

"Do you know what time the accident occurred?"

Nurse Cason moved to the foot of Katie's bed, lifted the chart, and flipped through the pages. "They put her into the helicopter at 10:27 a.m. and arrived here at 10:45 a.m. The only thing I can tell you is that the accident occurred before those times. My best guess would be that it happened between 9:00 and 9:30 this morning, but that is truly a guess. The police report can give you a more exact time."

"Thank you," Andy stammered. "Do you believe in magic?"

The nurse smiled. Andy thought her eyes twinkled as she said, "Oh, most assuredly. Magic and miracles are sometimes interchangeable." She offered Andy the drawstring bag and said, "Her clothes are a bit of a mess. I put them in the closet, along with her shoes. This bag contains her purse and jewelry. I thought you might want to take it along home with you."

Andy stood and took the bag. As she turned and left the room, he sat again in the chair next to his wife's bed and opened the bag. Whoever had packaged Katie's belongings had done so carefully. Her purse was wrapped in masking tape and placed inside a large zip topped bag. He opened the purse and found her jewelry in a separate bag. Katie's wedding and engagement rings were there, along with her watch and the emerald necklace she wore almost constantly. The necklace had been a first anniversary gift from him. Her watch was an old friend that she'd had longer than she'd known Andy.

Andy reached for Katie's old Timex watch, sad to see that the crystal had been smashed and the hands frozen. Katie would be sad to see the demise of the old timepiece. She had been wearing that wristwatch since her college days. She would be unhappy if it couldn't be repaired. Andy decided he would do whatever it took to get it back in working order, even if working order meant a new watch inside the original but beat-up casing. As Andy contemplated the condition of Katie's watch, he realized it had stopped at 9:17.

Andy remembered Katie had last phoned him at 9:20 that morning.

Now certain that his wife had been with him, Andy asked her again, "How do you do that?" He couldn't be certain, but thought he saw her eyebrow rise ever so slightly.

Andy spent the night in Katie's room, dozing in the chair by her bed, waking frequently to find nothing changed. When brilliant flashes of sunlight burst through the window and across his closed eyelids, he knew morning had arrived.

Daylight changed nothing. Katie looked exactly as she had before he had nodded off. He knew he would need to call Kathy. Thinking he should have told his daughter about her mother's accident the day before, he couldn't shake the feeling that he should still postpone the call.

Watching his wife, Andy thought about her belief that magic was simply a minor miracle, and that any miracle could be encouraged with faith and love. Yesterday had been both a nightmare and a miracle. He believed another miracle would follow. Again, he closed his eyes.

Andy awoke to the soft buzz of the alarm clock.

Automatically pushing the snooze button, Andy turned his head to the left and saw Katie sleepily smiling down at him. "Okay, I'm up and on my way to the studio," she whispered. "Go back to sleep. I am so looking forward to a day on the boat. If the weather is fit, maybe we can even spend the night out on the ocean. I'll see you on the dock by 8:30."

Andy looked at the clock. It was 3:30 a.m. As she always did on workdays, Katie would shower and dress and be on her way no later than 4:10 a.m., so she would arrive at the station by 4:30

a.m. to begin her weekday radio program, "Everyday Miracles".

Katie threw back the covers, then leaned down to her husband and kissed him soundly.

Andy gripped her wrist and said, "No. You can't go to the station today."

Surprised, and totally taken aback, Katie asked, "What are you talking about? I'll be done by 8:00 and we can be on our way by 9:00 at the latest."

"Kate, I want you to call off today. Tell them you're tired, or that a personal emergency has arisen, or whatever you need to do, but you can't go to the studio today." Andy's distress was apparent.

"You're serious, aren't you?" The obvious apprehension in her husband's voice concerned her.

Andy answered, "Please, Kate. I may be overreacting and ridiculous, but you live by your intuition and your plain old gut feelings. This is one of mine. Don't go to the studio today. Stay here with me."

Convinced her husband was truly reacting to a premonition, rather than his libido, she asked, "What is this all about?"

Somewhat embarrassed to admit his reasoning, Andy confessed, "I had a dream. It was so real that I'm afraid it was a forewarning. Please, Katie, don't go."

Katie saw the genuine terror in her husband's eyes. Ridiculous or not, she knew she couldn't refuse him. She said simply, "Okay."

Andy heaved a sigh of relief.

"I think this qualifies as a personal emergency," she said. "Besides, it will give us an earlier start."

Katie called the studio and explained that a personal situation required her presence. She had a few programs taped for those infrequent times that she was unavailable and was confident her absence would not be a problem.

Katie snuggled next to Andy. It would be nice to sleep a

few more hours. Andy draped his arm over his wife and fell into a deep and dreamless sleep.

A light sleeper, Katie was awakened a few hours later by the sound of sirens in the distance and the whop, whop, whop of a helicopter flying overhead. Andy was still sound asleep, which was not surprising. He could sleep through anything except an alarm clock.

Carefully throwing back the comforter, Katie slipped out of bed. She went downstairs to the kitchen to make coffee and turn on the news.

A reporter's image filled the television screen. With a sober expression, he reported, "Traffic on the interstate has been brought to a standstill after a dump truck lost its brakes near the top of Vine Street, and plunged down the hill across the intersection, and into the park. The truck swerved to miss a school bus, but smashed into the side of a taxi, before barreling onto the soccer field, which was soft and deep because of the recent rain. Though shaken up, the truck driver was not critically injured. The taxi driver was able to stagger away from the mangled cab, which luckily was not carrying a passenger at the time of the crash. He was taken to Trinity Hospital, where he was listed in stable condition."

A mangled taxi filled the screen.

How amazing that no one was killed, Katie thought. Vine Street was only a couple of blocks from her studio.

Katie turned from the television. The coffee was ready. She poured a cup, then walked out to the patio that overlooked the beach.

Katie smiled at the view she never tired of seeing. The roar of the ocean was continuous as the water swelled with each incoming wave, before collapsing on the sand, where the foamy liquid slid back to meet the next fluid peak, then repeated the process. The waves were endless, as the tides directed the rhythm of the saltwater's contact with the sand, as the sun climbed higher, illuminating the beach.

It was a gorgeous morning that promised clear weather. She and Andy would have a beautiful day.

###

Mountain Justice

Gravel scattered across the driveway as he braked his truck to a halt. She glanced out the window in time to see him lurch from the driver's seat. Trouble was coming. She went outside to meet him and cringed when he staggered up the steps to the porch. She saw his arm reach out. At the same time, a sudden pain jolted the side of her head, snapping her neck forward and knocking her to the maple planks of the splintered wooden floor.

He took two steps forward, reached for her right arm, pulled her to her feet, and said, "I saw you outside the grocery store with that veterinarian. I saw that look you gave him."

With her head pounding and her vision blurred, she pulled her arm backward, unsuccessful in her attempt to pull it from his grasp, and thought, "If I don't get away, this time he is going to kill me."

He hit her again. Her teeth punctured her lip and the familiar coppery taste of blood filled her mouth. She jerked her arm back and twisted away, breaking his grip. Somehow, she got to her feet and sprinted down the steps toward the road. He was right behind her.

In three long leaps, she was across the dirt road, past the fenced paddock and into the woods. Vaguely aware of a sharp pain in her shoulder, she was focused on the heavy steps that pounded close behind her. Running as fast as she could, she felt like she was slowing down and imagined she could feel his breath on her neck.

He was strong, and he could run, but she was faster. At least she had been before she was five months pregnant. She made it past the edge of the woods before she stopped to listen. Hidden by the width of the vast trunk of a giant old sycamore tree, she leaned against the tree to catch her breath. It was quiet. Had he turned back?

Before she could breathe a sigh of relief, she heard his slurred shout, "Don't think you can hide from me, sweetheart. I'll find you and make you sorry you ran."

If she could just stay hidden until morning, if she could just survive just once more, this time she would call the sheriff. It had to end. She slid her hands over the swell of her abdomen and whispered, "I'll protect you."

She felt his presence before the rustle of the underbrush announced him. She held her breath. He was close, perhaps no more than twenty feet away, but the crunch of the branches was softer, as though he were moving away from her, toward the stream. If he went down over the ridge, she could make it back to the barn and hide there until he passed out or left for the bar. She closed her eyes and prayed for him to keep moving. Then there was silence.

When she opened her eyes, he was standing five feet away. And when he reached for her, there was nowhere to run. With a grip like a vise, he grabbed her wrist. Without saying a word, he dragged her through the brush and the thorns, stumbling occasionally, but hanging onto her until they got back to the house.

After a brutal shove up the steps and across the porch, he said, "I told you not to run from me."

He kicked the front door open and thrust her into the house. She tripped and collapsed onto her knees. He pulled her to her feet, so that he could knock her down again, and again, and again.

***

A licensed veterinarian, Rob Tully lived alone. The nearest town was about twenty-five miles from his home, a log cabin that was surrounded by woods, near the top of the mountain. His family had lived on that mountain since 1882, when his great grandfather acquired one-hundred-seventy acres of land. Although the cabin had been expanded and renovated over the years, the original structure remained a part of the home.

As a child, Rob was taught that the mountain would provide just about everything a person needed. As an adult, Rob had found that to be true. Rob loved his mountain and the animals who shared it with him. He particularly liked to watch the vultures that flew above the cabin and roosted in the old walnut trees. Gramps always said they kept watch and let a person know if trouble was rolling in. Great Grandpa Tully had been an excellent teacher and Rob learned a lot from him, not only about nature but also about good vs. evil, and the wisdom of relying on what Gramps called 'gut instincts.' Some called them premonitions.

Beyond the ridge, the sun was making its slow ascent in the clear sky, and Rob expected a beautiful day. He was looking forward to seeing Annie later that morning. She had called and asked him to stop by and check on her horse in exchange for breakfast. He readily agreed. That woman certainly could cook.

Rob and Annie had been friends since childhood. Truth be told, he'd loved Annie since they were both about ten years old. He thought about the day they'd gone swimming. School was out for the summer and the weather was perfect for an afternoon at the lake. The grass was high, and billowed in the mild breeze, while the sun's warmth evaporated the lake water from their shoulders. They were racing up from the lake when Annie saw something move in the tall grass. She froze in her tracks and waited for another motion before she crept forward to see what was there.

"Oh, look, Robby! It's a garter snake!" Annie, being Annie, had no fear of any living creature. She carefully picked up the snake and held it up for Rob to see. At the time, he was amazed, not only at the colors of the snake, but that it was absolutely unafraid of Annie.

The snake looked at him and slowly moved around Annie's hand and lower arm. That's when ten-year-old Robby knew he was crazy about the red-headed snake charmer. He'd loved her ever since.

He was about to step into the shower when his pleasant thoughts of Annie were abruptly shoved aside and replaced with the memory of an August night over five years ago. A sense of imminent disaster accompanied the memory, much the same as he'd felt that night. Rob had been on his way home when something compelled him to stop at the McCutcheon farm.

Rob followed his impulse and turned down the lane to George and Annie's place. He parked next to their barn, and when he stepped down from the truck, Annie screamed. Rob didn't remember crossing the yard, leaping up the porch steps, or barreling through the front door, but he did remember seeing Annie. Bruised, bleeding, she had been cowering next to the refrigerator as George roughly took hold of her shoulders and began shaking her.

Rob had not said a word. He grabbed George from behind and threw him across the kitchen. The fight that followed resulted in Rob breaking a knuckle that still ached when it rained. Ultimately, he picked up a kitchen chair and knocked the drunken bully out cold before calling the police. Rob's intervention probably saved Annie's life. It also gave her the support she needed to press charges against her husband.

The police arrested George that night. Annie lost her baby two days later. George had gone to prison, and Annie filed for divorce. She had stayed on the farm, however, and somehow managed to keep it up by herself, although it was not unusual for Rob to help her with a lot of the heavy work. Like his mountain, Annie's farm had been in her family for generations, and she had no plan to move away.

Thinking back, Rob wondered, and not for the first time, if he should have killed George that night, but common sense had prevailed. George was sentenced to five years in prison. For what he'd done to Annie and her baby, five years sure didn't seem like justice.

Rob took a hasty shower and dressed quickly. Annie was an early riser, and he knew it wouldn't be a problem if he got there sooner than they had planned. He called her to tell her he'd be early, but she didn't answer. That was not a surprise. She was probably already out with the animals. On the way down the mountain, he'd try calling again.

***

Annie opened the door, looked across the yard toward the barn, and couldn't help smiling in appreciation of the beautiful morning. The sun's rays bounced off the dew-covered grass and glittered like the field was filled with tiny diamonds.

Rob would be on his way before long, and she wanted to get the morning chores done so they could relax over breakfast. Last night, she had called him and asked if he had time to stop by and take a look at her horse. Czar started acting up yesterday morning, and had been behaving strangely all day, which was not at all like him. Annie was afraid there could be something wrong that she wasn't able to see. Although Annie and Rob usually got together a couple of times a week, she was concerned enough about Czar that she didn't want to wait even one extra day. As always, she looked forward to seeing Rob. They had grown up together and were close friends. Although she'd never said it out loud, she'd loved him for years.

On her way to the barn, Annie's thoughts were interrupted when she heard Czar snorting and neighing in a high-pitched squeal that said something was wrong. She began to run, but wondered fleetingly if she should go back to the house for the shotgun just in case there was a cougar near the barn. Although large cats were uncommon in the area, they weren't unheard of. A loud thud told her Czar had started kicking at the wall of his stall, and that made the decision. Without going back for the shotgun, she ran even faster.

She unhooked the gate to the small paddock in front of the

barn. Closing the gate behind her, she quickly stepped to the barn and grabbed the pitchfork that was leaning against it. She held the pitchfork in her right hand, flung the sliding door open, and looked inside the barn. When the big stallion saw her, he pawed at the ground and began tossing his head. He was clearly angry.

Just inside the door, Annie stopped, and holding the pitchfork in front of her, did a quick look around the barn. Nothing seemed to be out of place. It was unusual that the two cats weren't perched somewhere waiting for her, but she figured Czar's antics could have frightened them. The cats were likely hiding by, waiting for him to settle down. She continued into the barn, walked directly to Czar's stall, hung the pitchfork on one of the hooks, and unlatched his gate.

"What's the matter, baby?" she crooned, opening the latch on the gate. "Why are you so upset?" Czar lowered his head and stepped closer to her. Annie reached her hand out, but before she could touch him, Czar threw his head back and reared up on his back legs. Surprised, Annie took a step back, at the same time that someone grabbed her left shoulder, spun her around, and slammed her against the stall, keeping the gate closed.

Before she could comprehend what was happening, a blow to the left side of her head blurred her vision and sent a pain shooting through her ear.

Oh, no, she thought. *This can't be happening again.* Before she could focus on who was doing this to her, the hand that had hit her came back in the other direction, connecting with the right side of her jaw. Giving her no time to react, the man grabbed her by the shoulders and slammed her into the stall gate. She remembered that combination, and was stunned as she thought, "*George has gotten out of prison and he is here to finish what he started five years ago.*"

Czar was furious. He stomped and snorted, circling in his stall. Annie turned and wrapped her fingers around the bars on the front of the gate. Her head was pounding and she could feel her eye beginning to swell. Sobbing involuntarily, she thought her only chance to escape this madman was to lock herself in the stall with Czar, but to do that, she had to pull the gate open and get past George.

"Cry all you want, sweetheart," George sneered. "You only ever got what you deserved back then, exactly like you will now. It wasn't enough that you sent me to jail, was it? You divorced me so that you and your boyfriend could live happily ever after. Did you really think I'd allow you to get away with that? Do you think that divorce means anything? You were my wife before I went to prison, and as far as I'm concerned, you're my wife now. I've had years to think about what I would do when I got out."

"No," she told him breathlessly, tightly gripping the bars of the stall gate with her back to him. She was fighting dizziness and her legs felt like rubber.

"Yes," he taunted. "I'll get you softened up a little more, and then we'll have ourselves a bunch of nice, long rolls in the hay. I've got to make up for a lot of lost time."

So, *he's going to beat me senseless and then rape me.* Out loud, she said, "don't do this. Please, George, just go away."

George clasped her shoulder again, but this time, pushed her into the bars, before he pulled her backwards toward him. Her fingers aching, Annie hung onto the gate as George tried to jerk her away from the stall.

Not realizing the gate to the stall had been unlatched, George didn't notice that by tugging on Annie, he was allowing the gate to open. His full attention was on his former wife and what he planned to do to her. George reached around her shoulders and grabbed Annie's wrists. He was trying to wrestle her hands from around the bars, when the gate opened far enough for Czar to discover he was no longer locked inside.

With his sights set on the man who had infuriated him, the enraged, half-ton, thoroughbred pushed the stall gate open and rushed out. George backed away from Annie when Czar came around the gate. He flattened himself against the wall to avoid the stallion's wrath as the horse charged toward him. Annie released her grip on the bars. In an effort to get around the gate and inside the stall, she moved in front of Czar. Then George saw the pitchfork on the other side of the barn. He tried to cross the shed row to reach it, but the horse reared up in front of him. To avoid razor sharp hooves, George moved back against the wall. The stallion's feet missed him by mere inches.

From inside the stall, Annie whistled before she collapsed onto the deep straw.

Czar's ears went up like they always did when he heard that sound. He spun around, moved quickly into his stall, and stopped in front of Annie. She struggled to her feet and used the horse's body for support as she reached for the gate. George crossed the barn and pulled the pitchfork from the hook. George turned and before Annie could close the gate from the inside, he pulled it open and went into the stall.

"Threaten me, will you?" George shouted, waving the pitchfork. "I should have shot you years ago," George snarled, advancing toward Czar. The stallion whirled around and faced George.

When Annie realized what George was going to do, it was sheer determination that forced her body from the corner of the stall. Her back was aching and her head was throbbing, but like a football tackle, she threw herself into George. When she hit him, her shoulder rammed his rib cage, which successfully knocked him several feet from where he had been menacing her horse. The effort, however, sapped all her strength. Again, she fell to the straw-covered floor, trembling and breathing heavily.

With a roar, George was back on his feet, turning the pitchfork toward Annie, as she crab-walked backward to get away from him. As if he understood what was about to happen, Czar reared up and came down fast. His right hoof struck George's shoulder and knocked the pitchfork to the ground. George landed on top of it. Czar reared up a second time, clearly trying to finish the battle, but George was fast and threw himself across the stall toward the corner where Annie was huddled. Again, he avoided the horse's hooves.

With his left shoulder fractured, George tried to pull Annie in front of him, using only his right arm. She twisted away and, with a surge of adrenaline, fought him to the best of her ability. She finally connected with a hard kick to his knee, which she was certain caused some damage, but more importantly, it allowed her to shove him back toward the center of the stall, and away from her.

Through it all, the horse had continued to stomp and spin, and when Annie gave George that final push, Czar's aim was perfect. As his feet came down, he hit George again. His left hoof only grazed George's shoulder, but when Czar's right foot came down, it hit George on the side of his head, slicing his scalp and tearing the top of his ear. This time, George stayed down.

"Whoa, Czar," Annie called to the horse. "Good boy," she said shakily. "Settle down now." She stumbled to her feet and stepped next to the horse. He put his head down, nuzzling her hand. She heard Rob's truck coming up the road just before she passed out.

***

Rob pulled onto the McCutcheon's long driveway, slowly making his way over the ruts and the rocks to the barn where he was planning to meet Annie and check on Czar. He hadn't been able to reach her, and while it wasn't unusual for Annie to be away from the phone, he couldn't shake the feeling that something was terribly wrong. He was certain the problem was with Czar and Rob was afraid something had happened to the stallion.

Annie had raised that horse from the time he was four months old. Czar was Annie's buddy. He was a stallion, and as is the nature of many stallions, he could be a tough guy. He followed

Annie around, however, like a duckling following his mother. The two of them were a joy to watch. Czar responded to her every whim and Annie clearly adored him. If anything happened to him, she would be devastated.

Rob was probably the only other person who could easily handle the horse. Though Czar was, in most cases, relatively cooperative with Rob, it was not always an uneventful exchange. Rob had been stepped on more than once, though Czar never kicked him. The horse did, however, bruise him pretty colorfully with an occasional bite on the shoulder, particularly if Annie got close when Rob was tending to him.

Rob parked the car next to the paddock outside the barn. It surprised him that Annie wasn't waiting in the paddock. She usually met him outside when she heard the truck. Rob opened the gate and, as he turned to close it, he was startled by the sound of hooves moving swiftly toward him. Spinning around, he saw the open barn door, and Czar charging toward him.

"Whoa, Czar! Easy, boy," he told the oncoming horse, holding his arms up over his head. "Whoa, now."

Apparently recognizing Rob, Czar stopped about two feet from him, stomping his front foot, and throwing his head. Nostrils flared, and with his ears pinned back against his head, the horse was more than upset. He was angry.

Where is Annie?

"Annie?" Rob had called, keeping his eyes on Czar and reaching out toward him. Czar's ears pricked at the sound of her name.

"Easy, Czar," Rob said, his left hand stroked the horse's jaw. "What are you doing out here by yourself? Where's Annie?"

Czar tossed his head, then turned and trotted into the barn.

"Annie?" Rob called again before following Czar through the barn door.

Czar went directly to his stall. The gate was open.

"Good boy," Rob said, planning to lock him in the stall,

and then figure out why Annie wasn't around.

As suddenly as the stallion had calmed down in the paddock, he became furious at the entrance to his stall. With a shake of his head, he reared up and thundered his front hooves down, then began to paw at the straw covered floor.

"Down, Czar, take it easy, son. Whoa, now. What's going on here?" Rob kept talking as he slowly approached the irritated stallion.

Rob wanted Czar to go forward a couple more feet, so that he could get the gate closed and the horse safely locked in the stall, before searching for Annie. It was unheard of for Czar to be loose without Annie close by him, and so she couldn't be far away.

Czar moved a couple of steps into his stall. In two long strides, Rob got to the gate but stopped abruptly when he saw the problem inside.

In the center of the stall, a man was on his hands and knees. The man's clothes were as bloody as his face. He'd been crawling toward the gate, probably trying to close Czar out of the stall, but the stallion would not allow it.

Czar reared up again, and though his front hooves missed the man's head by a fraction of an inch, one hoof stuck his back, knocking him to the ground. Rob cringed at the thought of the pain that must have caused and wondered if the blow had broken a bone. Rob knew he needed to stop the stallion before he killed the man in the stall.

Grabbing a rope which was hanging from the gate, Ron entered the stall. He threw the rope over Czar's shoulder, and reached under his neck to close the loop, so he could turn the horse away from the man and move him out of the stall. That's when he saw Annie curled up in the front corner of the enclosure. Her shirt was torn and her lip was bleeding. Her eyes were closed, and she wasn't moving.

Czar lowered his head menacingly and took a step toward the man, who cowered along the side of the stall. Giving the rope a two-handed tug, Rob hollered at the furious stallion, "Stop! Settle down!"

Startled, yet responsive, Czar turned with Rob, but took only a single step, before kicking back with his rear legs. Rob heard the horse's hooves make contact with the body of the man in the stall. He shuddered at the sound of the thud when Czar's feet came down with what Ron was certain had been a solid hit.

Rob quickly led Czar to the adjoining stall and locked him inside. Turning back, Rob moved past the man, who had collapsed along the side of the stall, and reached for Annie. The moaning man would have to wait. Dropping to his knees next to her, Rob could see Annie taking short, quick breaths. At least she was breathing.

"Annie?" he whispered. "Annie, can you hear me?"

Annie opened her right eye and focused on Rob. With her left eye swollen closed, she looked past Rob. She focused her gaze on Czar before she locked her eyes on Rob's.

"Robby," she stammered. "George was waiting for me in the barn. He must have been around here yesterday. That's why Czar was acting strangely."

"George," Rob repeated. "That man is George? Did he do this to you?"

Annie nodded her head.

Rob watched the big stallion who was standing calmly, quietly observing Annie through the bars. She looked up at Czar and made two soft kissing sounds. The stallion pricked his ears and whinnied quietly.

Annie's first tears fell silently, but the silence quickly gave way to heartbreaking sobs as she reached up to put her arms around Rob's neck. Rob hugged her to his chest and told her, "I need to see if George is alive. Then you're going to tell me what happened. Can you stand up?"

Again, she nodded.

Rob helped Annie to her feet and walked her to the other

side of the barn, where he sat her on a bench. When he turned to go back and find out George's condition, she gripped his arm. Clasping it, with both of her hands, she said, "They'll call Czar a killer and take him away from me. People will never believe he did it to save my life."

Still clutching his arm, she continued, "George started hitting me. Czar knew I was in trouble. I was right outside his stall. I opened the gate and went inside with him. George grabbed the pitchfork and followed me. He tried to stab my horse. Czar went crazy and attacked him. Czar was protecting me."

She stopped and took a deep, but shaky, breath before she continued, "I didn't try to stop him, Robby. I wanted Czar to kill him. But now, I'm afraid that if George dies, they will label Czar a killer. He'll be destroyed, but he's not a killer. He did it to save my life."

"Wait here," Rob told her.

He walked back to Czar's stall, and looked at George McCutcheon, who was crumpled in a heap on the straw. Rob felt no compassion. George didn't appear to be breathing, so Rob dropped to one knee and felt for a pulse. It was there, though faint. His breathing was shallow and irregular. If George died, Annie was right, Czar would be destroyed. Even if George lived, the stallion would probably be determined to be dangerous and could still receive a mandate for destruction. But what terrified Rob even more was that he knew if George lived, Annie would never be safe from him.

Rob went back to Annie and sat on the bench next to her. "Look at me, Annie," he told her. "No matter what happens, and no matter who asks, you need to forget that George was ever here. You haven't seen George since before he went to prison. Do you understand?"

Annie studied Rob's eyes for a minute before responding. She said simply, "Yes."

Unsteady, but determined, she stood and walked calmly

toward her horse.

"What are we going to do?" she asked.

"We aren't going to do anything," Rob told her. "I am going to take care of the problem."

He reached out, cupped her chin in his hand, and said, "George was never here."

Rob picked up a saddle blanket and re-entered the stall. George moaned once. His breathing was uneven. Rob was certain that George would die without immediate medical attention, but he had no intention of providing it. His intention was to expedite George's entry into the next world.

Rob kneeled next to the unconscious man. He covered George's face with the saddle blanket, pressed it firmly against his nose and mouth. George didn't struggle, and for that, Rob was grateful. It took less than a minute for his breathing to stop, but Rob kept pressure on the blanket and held it in place a little while longer. Rob never doubted that what he was doing was the right thing.

When he was sure George was dead, Rob stood, closed his eyes, and prayed for forgiveness. Annie walked up behind him. She wrapped her arms around Rob's neck and placed her cheek against his shoulder. Closing her eyes, she murmured, "You always take care of me, Robby." She turned away from Rob and went into the stall with Czar.

Rob hoisted George up over his shoulder, carried him to the truck, and situated him under a blanket in the truck bed. He slowly drove back to the mountain.

When Rob got home, he went to the walnut grove near the mountain peak. He carefully lifted the body from the bed of the truck and carried it to the ridge, where he gently placed George's body under the walnut trees. Rob said a prayer for the dead man's immortal soul.

Rob walked back to the house and watched the vultures from a distance. They were circling and diving near the old walnut trees. He knew it was only a matter of hours before George's bones would be picked clean by the scavengers. It would be a matter of days before the bones were scattered across the mountain, dragged by wild animals, or even stray dogs, to be devoured at their leisure.

He got back into his truck and drove down the mountain road, back to Annie's farm. He didn't think she had any broken bones, but he wanted to be sure she hadn't been more seriously injured than it appeared. She should also keep ice on her eye, and he knew she wouldn't do it if he wasn't there to watch her.

As he was driving, Rob thought about what had happened. In his mind, he went over what he had done and why he had done it. He decided that justice doesn't necessarily adhere to the mandates of the legal system. While we would prefer that to be the case, sometimes it simply isn't possible. What is most important is that justice triumphs. Today, it did.

Forever

"Denny," she said as he was closing the door, "I heard something upstairs."

"It was probably Simon climbing up the bookshelves again." Denny laughed. At the sound of his name, Simon responded with a quiet meow.

"It wasn't Simon. He's right here," Andrea whispered. She lifted the kitten from the floor. "Denny, what if someone broke into the house?"

Denny heard the fear in Andrea's voice. Although he wasn't convinced there was someone inside, Denny moved in front of Andrea, and waited motionless, listening for any sound. He did not turn on the light.

Denny was a big guy, confident and in relatively good physical shape, for a forty-five-year-old man. There wasn't much that frightened or intimidated him. Although he was irritated at the thought that someone had broken into his house, he was doubtful that it was anything he couldn't handle.

"Stay here with Simon," Denny whispered. "I'll see what's going on. I'm sure it's nothing." He kissed Andrea softly, then gave Simon a light scratch under the chin before moving quietly through the kitchen and into the dining room. He stepped into the hallway, not expecting to see the masculine silhouette approaching him from the staircase.

At the same time Denny saw him, the man rushed at Denny. Denny crouched and threw a block like he did back in his college days when he'd played right tackle. When Denny hit him, the intruder fell back and slammed into the wall.

"Andrea, get out of the house," Denny yelled as he reached toward the hall table for the brass lamp, "and call the police."

The man came at him again, but Denny saw the knife in his

hand.

The intruder brandished the knife like a sword, but Denny swung the lamp, ripping the lamp's cord from the wall outlet and connecting with the burglar's forearm.

The burglar took a step back, without losing his grip on the knife. Denny swung the lamp up to the right, aiming for the intruder's jaw, but the loose lamp cord caught on the table leg, pulling the table into Denny's left leg and slowing the lamp's progress.

With lightning speed, the intruder pushed Denny to the floor and straddled him. Left forearm across Denny's chest, the burglar raised his right hand, still holding the knife. Denny grabbed the man's wrist, and with a straight arm, he deflected the knife. When he heard Andrea gasp, he wondered why she was still in the house.

"Get out of the house, Andy," Denny hollered, using all his strength to keep the knife from penetrating his body.

"Leave him alone," he heard Andrea scream, and he watched in horror as she threw herself onto the startled man.

The prowler was incredibly quick. He rolled onto his back, grabbed Andrea, and pulled her on top of him. With one arm around her ribs and the other around her neck, he dragged her with him as he used his legs to push himself away from Denny and his back to slide up the wall until standing, holding Andrea in front of himself.

Denny scrambled onto his feet but didn't dare reach for the man who had a knife within inches of Andrea's throat.

The prowler screamed at Denny, "Stay there. I'm leaving. She's coming with me. If you follow me, I will cut her throat."

Crying, Andrea whimpered, "I'm so sorry, Denny. I called the police, but I couldn't stay outside. I was afraid for you. I love you."

It was then Denny saw the blood pooling at her feet that she must have gotten cut when she attacked the intruder. He wondered if she even realized she was bleeding. There was so much blood, but he knew if he moved toward her, the attacker would cut her throat.

"The police are on the way," Denny said, as calmly as he could manage, looking directly into the intruder's eyes. "Leave now. Release my wife and just leave. I won't try to stop you."

"She's coming with me," the man said, and, without taking his eyes from Denny, he backed toward the door.

Andrea's eyes rolled up, and she went limp.

"Look at the floor," Denny said. "She's bleeding to death." Then he yelled, "Please, just let her go!"

The burglar looked down and saw pooling blood. He hesitated before shoving her at Denny, then pivoted and ran out of the house.

Denny caught Andrea and lowered her to the floor. He ran to the kitchen and brought back towels to try to stop the bleeding. The blood was streaming from her lower abdomen. He pressed the towels to the knife wound and pleaded with her, "Andy, don't leave me. You stay with me. Open your eyes. Andrea, open your eyes and look at me."

Her eyelids fluttered. She smiled at him, then closed her eyes and stopped breathing the moment the police arrived.

The police immediately began artificial respiration while Denny continued to keep pressure on the wound. They couldn't save her.

"Andrea!" Denny awoke, crying. His heart was pounding and perspiration dripped from his forehead. The dream had come again.

It was June 25th, the third anniversary of Andrea's murder. The entire incident played through his mind in vivid detail, as it did last June 25th and the June 25th before that. Though he missed Andrea every day of his life, he only had the dream of reliving her death of three years ago on June 25th, her birthday.

They never found her killer.

Simon rubbed against Denny's left ear, purring and sounding like a miniature motorcycle. It seemed like the cat was trying to distract Denny from the horror of the dream. It was as though Simon truly understood what Denny was thinking. Simon had been Denny's Christmas present to Andrea the year before her death and had been his constant companion since she died.

"Simon," he smiled at the cat. "I think you still miss her, too, huh? Let's get some breakfast, you fur ball."

Denny ambled out to the kitchen. Simon followed but stopped in the dining room. The cat curled up next to the chair by the window, purring louder than usual.

Andrea had loved to sit in that chair, drinking coffee in the morning and watching the rabbits play in their backyard.

While the coffee was brewing, Denny returned to the living room and turned on the television. A news alert was being broadcast. A familiar reporter was speaking. "An unidentified man was found stabbed in the subway. If you have any information about this incident, or if you know this man, please contact the police."

The television screen filled with a picture of a man whose image Denny would never forget. It was the man who had killed Andrea.

Denny stared at the image. He felt like someone had punched him in the stomach and knocked the wind out of him. Taking a deep breath, he looked again. Andrea's killer was dead. He sat down, staring at the picture on the television screen, but not hearing any of the words being said.

He imagined he heard laughter. Yes, Andrea, he thought. The bastard surely got what he deserved, but you certainly didn't.

He wondered if he should call the police, then decided it no longer mattered. The police had tried but had been unsuccessful in finding the killer. Someone else had found him. As far as Denny was concerned, it was over. The killer had paid and wouldn't hurt anyone else ever again. Denny was good with that. He could stop searching. He could stop looking at every dark-haired, middle-aged man he saw on the street, on a bus, on the subway, in restaurants, grocery stores, banks and everywhere he went.

Denny went back to the kitchen and poured a cup of coffee, then returned to the dining room and Andrea's chair. Sullen, he gazed out through the window in search of rabbits.

Acting like a cat possessed, Simon was running in circles, jumping in the air and batting at something only he could see.

"Simon, you are a silly cat." Denny laughed as he watched the cat rolling on the floor and rubbing up against the leg of the chair.

Simon ignored Denny and continued playing with nothing. Simon could make Denny smile when nothing else could.

After a few minutes, Denny stood and called to the cat. "Come on, Simon. It's time to take a shower." Simon usually followed Denny to the shower, no doubt wondering if it was safe to be that close to so much water. It was a morning ritual.

Simon looked at Denny, got up, and followed until a toy mouse appeared from nowhere. Simon pounced on the mouse, threw it up into the air and, when it hit the floor, he pounced again. He rolled with the mouse and then dashed to the corner of the dining room, where he started purring again and rubbing the leg of Andrea's chair.

For the second time that morning, Denny imagined he heard laughter, only louder and closer. It sounded like it was right next to him. He turned and looked back toward the kitchen.

"Did I leave the television on?" Denny asked the cat. Then he saw her.

Andrea stood next to her dining room chair, looking exactly as she had on the last day of her life. She was wearing her favorite jeans and her soft white sweater, still the most beautiful woman Denny had ever seen.

"Hey, Denny," she greeted, her voice as clear as when she had been alive.

Denny stared at his wife. He knew she couldn't be there, yet there she was.

"You can see me, can't you? Simon can see me. He can hear me, too. Can you hear me, Denny?" Andrea smiled.

Denny simply stared at the translucent image of Andrea.

"I killed him," Andrea told him.

Confused, Denny took a step toward Andrea, his sweet, gentle Andrea wondering, *How is it possible that she is speaking to me? Am I looking at my wife and hearing that she killed her murderer?*

"His name was Aaron," she continued. "A long time ago, when we were just children, he was my best friend. He lived next door. We went to the same school. We did everything together. When we graduated from high school, we got married. It was what everyone expected. Things changed then. Aaron became jealous and possessive. I left him. He threatened me. I divorced him. For a while, he stalked me. Then he just disappeared. I left Colorado and moved out here. I started a new life. That's when I met you. I never dreamed I would ever see him again. I never imagined he was still trying to find me. It was as though he was dead. I told you I was a widow because I felt like a widow. I'm so sorry, Denny."

"Andy," Denny said. "I can see you and I can talk to you. How is that possible?"

"I never left you, Denny," she told him. "It took a while for me to channel enough energy to try to communicate. Then I had to learn to focus on the energy and direct it. Simon could sense me right away, and sometimes I thought you could, too, but I was never sure. You know all those light bulbs that kept blowing out? That was me." She laughed. "At first, I was afraid Aaron would come back, so I stayed to try to protect you. Then I saw Aaron at my funeral and I followed him. I watched him until I was sure he wouldn't bother you."

"You were at your funeral?" Denny asked.

"Yes. I had a choice to stay or leave," she explained. "I

chose to stay. I couldn't leave you, and I hoped that one day I could let you know I was still here."

Denny moved toward Andrea. "I'm sorry I couldn't protect you. It's my fault you died. I didn't take care of you."

Andrea shook her head. "You always took care of me. If I had done what you said that night and stayed outside, things might have been different, but I was afraid he was going to kill you. I couldn't have lived with that. The more time that passed, the more I learned about moving from place to place and how to channel energy." Andrea stopped talking and began to disappear, but a few seconds later, her image returned. She continued, "I also found that I could make suggestions to some people and they would think the suggestions were their own ideas."

"Did you do that with me?" Denny asked her.

"Never," she stated firmly. "I would never want you to do anything that wasn't totally and absolutely you. It was different with Aaron, though. As I said, I followed him from my funeral to where he was living. He had some friends who were easy to direct. I practiced with them. It took me a long time to get to when I knew I had control, then I directed one of them to kill him. I won't tell you who killed him, but I will tell you they will never find his killer, and the killer doesn't remember killing him."

"How long can you stay here like this?" Denny asked her. "Can you come and go or appear at will?"

"I'm really not sure," Andrea replied. "I can see you almost all the time. Simon usually knows when I'm here, but not always. I will stay as long as you want me to stay, as long as I'm able to stay."

Denny stepped closer to her and said, "Andy, I have missed you so much." He reached to take her hand and, though he could see her, he couldn't touch her.

"It's finally over, Denny," she told him. "I killed Aaron for you and for me, and now I've come back home."

Simon looked up at Andrea but arched his back and

lowered his ears. He hissed like Denny had never heard him hiss before.

"What's the matter, Simon?" Denny asked. "It's Andrea. You know that." Simon was staring past Andrea toward the kitchen door.

Andrea turned and Denny moved to her side. Denny heard her gasp before he saw the man, who he recognized as Aaron, walk rapidly toward them.

"Yes, my treacherous beauty," Aaron said, "you are home, and so am I." Aaron took Andrea's hand and, as they both slowly faded into a mist, Denny heard Aaron say, "You had no right to leave me in life, because you belong to me, and we are meant to be together."

"But as long as I was alive, I couldn't be with you. Having me killed changed that. We can be together again now. You were mine in life, Andrea, and now you are mine, again, in death, where we will stay together, and this time forever."

###

Indisputable Evidence

Uncertain what had awakened her, Melissa glanced at the clock. It was 3:32 a.m. She reached for Michael but found that she was alone. Sometimes he was restless in the early morning hours. When that happened, he'd often take a short walk around the property. Melissa supposed she had heard the door slap shut as Michael left the warm house to enjoy the cool night air. He was never gone for very long.

Yawning widely, Melissa stretched, then closed her eyes and hoped for another four hours of sleep. She was drifting back into oblivion when she heard a sharp cracking sound, followed by the musical crashing of broken glass lightly, but plentifully hitting the hardwood floor in the room below.

Melissa and Michael had lived in Ellsworth for three years. Their home was located in a lovely, secluded spot along the water, a beautiful old estate that overlooked the rocky Atlantic coast. On vacation in New England, Melissa had spied the *For Sale* sign while taking photographs of the cliff at the edge of the property. It was love at first sight.

Melissa was a photographer who preferred solitude to the hustle bustle of the city, or even the suburbs. The property for sale in Ellsworth was certainly off the beaten path, secluded but easily within biking distance to reach a complete community. When she saw the stone wall rising gracefully from the top of the bluff, she'd imagined workmen finding just the right stones along the rocky cliffs, then carting them to the property, until enough stones accumulated into mounds. It must have taken months, or even years, to create the three-foot wall along the property's edge.

The wall overlooked a cliff that fell to the rocky coastline of the ocean below. Though easily scaled from inside the perimeter, the wall provided some protection against an accidental plunge to almost certain injury and possibly even death. A tall iron fence met the stones on either end, surrounding the estate to project a mysterious, yet reassuring feeling of safety.

Inside the old house, Melissa had found further delights. She adored the cherry-mahogany wood trim that framed the doors and windows, and the stone floor in the entryway. The kitchen had an ancient brick oven. Fueled with wood, or maybe coal, the old cook-stove took up an enormous area in the corner of the enormous kitchen, but Melissa had no intention of changing anything.

Melissa was enchanted by the ornately framed painting that hung above the fireplace. Someone had obviously created it many years prior. It portrayed a middle-aged man seated on a velvet loveseat with his arm wrapped around a dark-haired woman. A jet-black Newfoundland lounged on the floor at their feet.

Surprised at what she considered a low sale price, Melissa had asked the real estate agent how such an exquisite property had gone unsold for over two years.

Looking directly into Melissa's eyes, with no hint of a smile, he replied. "It's haunted."

"Haunted?" She laughed. "People believe the house is truly haunted?"

The agent nodded grimly. "Bernard MacNellis built the original house in 1803. The story is that Bernard was out on his fishing boat early one afternoon when an unexpected storm blew in. It was a bad one, with high winds and lightning. Though no one knows for sure, the authorities believed that when that storm was threatening, Bernard's wife, Sophia, went out on the cliffs to look for his boat. Since the stone wall wasn't complete, it would have been easy to step too close to the edge of the cliff. They suspect the wind caught Sophia's cape with enough force to pull her from the cliff and onto the rocks below."

The realtor paused to catch his breath. "When Bernard returned home, the storm was at its height. Sophia wasn't in the house and Bernard's old dog, Mason, was outside, barking and carrying on frantically at the edge of the rocky coast. Bernard found Sophia. She had fallen to her death."

The realtor pulled a handkerchief from his pants pocket, carefully unfolded it, and wiped his glasses before continuing.

"Bernard was inconsolable. No matter what the weather, he and Mason walked the cliff's edge every night for months. He told his friends he was walking with Sophia. It was six months to the day when they found Bernard and the old dog at the bottom of the cliff, in the same place Sophia had died. They say Bernard and Sophia both stayed here on the grounds," the agent said. "She couldn't leave Bernard. When he followed her to the grave, both of them stayed right here."

"I seriously doubt that there are such things as ghosts among us." Melissa told him. She was open-minded about most things, but at thirty-one years old, she had yet to see a ghost, or any convincing evidence of their existence.

The realtor continued, somewhat sadly, "I think it's only right that potential buyers know the history of the estate, although it surely hasn't been a selling point."

Melissa slowly nodded. "I can see where rumors of ghosts could be a liability."

When Melissa returned to the hotel, she found Michael lounging on the bed. Together, they went back to the estate. They spent the rest of the day wandering the grounds and the rock-strewn coast. She loved the property, and he loved the property. Michael was fascinated by the stone wall. He kept wandering to the spot that overlooked the cliff and stood silently gazing at the rocks below.

They moved into the house a month later. They had yet to meet Bernard or Sophia, but Melissa loved the painting of the two of them with their dog, and she kept it hanging above the fireplace.

After a long day, Melissa had gone to bed early. She was almost asleep when she heard what sounded like a glass breaking.

"Okay, Melissa, don't panic," she told herself silently. "*Maybe Bernard and Sophia making their presence known*," although she didn't believe that for a moment. She listened intently.

The sound of falling glass had morphed into the echo of crunching glass, followed by a few heavy footsteps, then nothing. Someone was in the house. Careful to move as quietly as possible, Melissa slipped out of bed. When her feet hit the cold floor, she reached for her moccasins, grateful for the insulation as they hugged her feet. She was wearing a pair of warm flannel pajamas and decided not to take time to cross the room for her robe.

Melissa picked up her cell phone, which was on the top of the nightstand by the bed. She pushed nine-one-one. Nothing happened. She tried twice before she realized she had no service. Life away from the mainstream had many advantages, but one disadvantage was an inconsistent cell phone connection.

Melissa considered locking herself in the bedroom. If she did that, the burglar could steal what he wanted, then maybe he would just leave and she could let the insurance company worry about the damage. Locked in the bedroom, however, she had no way to call for help. She could become a prisoner with someone wandering through her house for days. Of even more concern was that if she was locked in the bedroom, Michael would be locked outside of it.

"Melissa, get yourself together," she told herself. "*The cell service is better at the foot of the stairs. Get there and dial nine-one-one."*

Calmer, now that she had a plan, she continued the conversation with herself. "*Even if you don't speak to someone, if you connect with a dispatcher, they'll send help."* Again, she wondered, *"Where was Michael?"*

Concerned that Michael could be in trouble, Melissa slipped through the half-open bedroom door and into the hall.

The house was dark, but the moon was close to full. The bright moonlight came through the windows and allowed her to see reasonably well. She crept toward the top of the staircase, but stopped when she heard a masculine voice call softly, "Ed? Eddy?" Unable to be sure exactly where the voice was coming from, Melissa took a few steps backward.

"Eddy, are you in here?" The voice was directly below her.

She held her breath and listened, then she saw a man ascending the staircase toward the bedroom.

"Oh, no. Now what do I do?" Melissa didn't dare move. She tried to melt into the wall, and thought, "I *need a weapon.*"

Then she remembered. She had a weapon. The old sword she'd found in the attic was leaning up against the wall, about ten feet to her left. She had planned to hang it above the table at the head of the stairs. In order to get to the sword, she would have to cross the staircase, which meant that Eddy's companion would almost definitely see her. The sword, however, could be a formidable weapon. She had to reach it.

The man coming up the stairs didn't appear to be much bigger than her own five-foot-seven-inch, one-hundred-and-sixty-pound frame. He had one hand on the railing and the other at his side. It looked like his hands were empty. Melissa was confident that she could mount a reasonable defense, particularly since the intruder would never expect to meet an irate woman armed with a Revolutionary War sword.

Melissa turned to her left. She focused on the table, knowing the sword was on the opposite side. *"Okay, Melissa,* she thought, *take a deep breath, focus. Go now!"*

She passed the head of the stairs at the same time the burglar reached the top step. Both of them moved forward quickly and with purpose.

Melissa was in good shape and fast, but the prowler was

faster. She got to the table, but before Melissa could grab the sword, she was hit squarely between the shoulder blades and fell to the floor, the weight of the invader on her back.

"Why didn't you stay in your room, you stupid bitch? Now, look what you've done. Damn it. Damn you," he said, breathing heavily.

Melissa coughed and tried to breathe. She panted, "I have money downstairs. I'll get it. Then you can just leave." Her mind was racing. "*Michael, where are you? Have they done something to you?*"

The man flipped Melissa onto her back and sat on her thighs. With his hands, he pinned her forearms to the floor. "Sure, Honey. I'll leave and then you can call the cops and tell them all about my pretty face."

"No," Melissa said, getting her breathing under control. "It's dark. I can't see you." She turned her head to the side to avoid looking at him, tears beginning to form. "*I will not allow this bastard to get away with this.*"

The man pulled her arms from her sides and raised them above her head. He grasped both wrists in his right hand. He was stronger than he looked. With his left hand, he unbuckled his belt, unbuttoned his jeans and reached for his zipper.

Melissa screamed and fought her would be rapist with everything she had, still intent on reaching the sword. She bucked and twisted and kept screaming, while trying to slide her body closer to the table.

"Make all the noise you want, baby. I like noise."

"I'll castrate you, you weasel," she silently vowed, while she continued to back-kick the man above her. She was within inches of the sword.

Though he still had her arms pinned over her head, her gyrations had caused him to use both of his hands to hold her arms in place. Melissa felt certain that she could twist her body to break his grip. The question was whether she could grab that old sword and swing it quickly enough, even if it meant killing him.

"I won't know until I try," she thought. "*Doing nothing sure isn't an option."*

It was then that she heard the familiar three thumps on the stairs.

Before she had time to call Michael's name, the man on top of her was knocked to the side and covered by the furious German Shepherd who was snapping and biting, intent on protecting his mistress.

"What the hell? Stop! Get him off me," her attacker hollered.

Melissa rolled away from them and grabbed the sword. "Michael. Come here," she commanded.

Michael stopped snapping but wouldn't move away from the would-be rapist. Panting and snarling, the dog growled, low and steady, his muzzle three inches from the man's throat. He stared into the man's eyes while his low, menacing rumble continued.

Melissa was relieved to see Michael alive and well, and she was no longer the least bit frightened. She was, however, absolutely furious. She was in control now and determined to put the bastard behind bars.

"Keep in mind he has a friend," she reminded herself when she recalled he had been calling for Eddy.

Melissa hoped Michael had previously found Eddy, whoever he might be, and had sent him back over the wall or under the gate and off the property. That would explain Michael's prior absence. It would also explain why Eddy was apparently not where this jerk had expected to meet him.

"You no good creep," she said, her voice low and menacing. "My dog would like nothing better than to tear out your throat, and I'm tempted to let him do it."

While Michael didn't like or dislike tearing out throats, she hoped her claim would terrify her assailant. The dog had never attacked anyone before, but then he'd never had reason to.

"I have my dog under control, but only as long as he believes I am safe," Melissa warned. "If he thinks I am in danger, he makes his own decisions."

"Just get him away from me. I think the son of a bitch broke my hand. I know he took a chunk out of my arm. I'm going to bleed to death," the man blubbered.

"I have got to call the police. What am I going to do with this guy?" Melissa thought. She saw her cell phone where she had dropped it a couple of feet away. She stepped around Michael and picked it up, without taking her eyes off the intruder. There was still no signal.

"I need to go downstairs to get to the land phone," she thought. *"But I'm not going anywhere without Michael, so we've got to take this jerk downstairs with us."*

"Michael, here, come here, baby," Melissa whispered. The dog reluctantly turned and went to her. Melissa pulled his head to her side and scratched his ears.

"Good boy; you are such a wonderful boy," she told him. His tail wagged briefly. "We aren't done yet."

She pointed to the cowering man, "Watch him, Michael." Melissa's companion, turned bodyguard, focused his attention on the burglar, though this time, not making a sound.

"Okay, get on your feet and do it slowly, or I swear, I'll let this dog tear you apart," Melissa told the intruder as she turned on the hall lamp.

The man's right hand hung limply. Melissa figured Michael had broken it. Blood seeped from his arm where it looked like the dog had bitten him more than once, but it didn't appear to be bleeding excessively.

"Turn around and walk toward the stairs." Melissa pointed the sword at the man's back and gave him a nudge with the pointed blade. It was all she could do to resist sliding the blade straight through his body. Michael was at her side, his eyes on the man in front of them.

"Look, Miss, I'm sorry. I wasn't going to hurt you. I just wanted to scare you. I would never …"

"Shut up," Melissa interrupted. "Just shut the hell up and put your hands behind your back." Alert to the tension in Melissa's voice, Michael growled. The prowler put his hands behind his back.

Melissa opened the small drawer in the hall table and pulled out two braided drapery ties. She put the sword on the tabletop and carefully approached the man.

"I'm going to tie your hands. If you make any move, my dog will attack you." The man seemed to have stopped breathing.

Melissa carefully tied his wrists tightly together with one of the drapery ties, and then tied them again with the other. He flinched slightly as she tightened the makeshift hand cuffs.

She retrieved the sword. "Now start down the stairs," she demanded.

He walked to the staircase and slowly descended, with Melissa and Michael close behind. When they reached the bottom of the stairs, Melissa ordered, "Turn right."

At the same time Melissa pushed up the wall switch for the overhead lamp, a gunshot exploded, the flash briefly illuminated the kitchen. Her captive groaned and called out, "Eddy! It's me, Mitch." He dropped to his knees. "Don't shoot."

Michael barked and raced into the dark kitchen, as Melissa hollered, "Michael, no, stay with me!" Her command was too late.

His barking intensified to a near roar, and the one called Eddy screamed. There was a second flash as another bullet exploded from the weapon. Then there was silence.

Melissa stepped over the groaning Mitch, and raced into the kitchen, unmindful that more bullets could be aimed in her direction. All she could think about was Michael. She held the sword like a baseball bat, ready to swing it toward anyone in her path.

The moonlight poured through the kitchen windows, illuminating a scene that she would remember for the rest of her life. On the floor of the kitchen, she saw a large, dark-haired man lying on his back at the foot of the huge stone oven, with Michael's ninety-pound body sprawled across his chest. A gun was on the floor to the right of the man's arm. The assailant's jacket was mangled, torn at the shoulder, and ripped down the side. Michael must have knocked Eddy backward, which caused the gunman's head to collide with the huge stone oven, but not before he'd been able to shoot the fearless dog.

Melissa switched on the kitchen light. Keeping the sword in front of her, she took three cautious steps toward them, then lowered the sword, touching the point to the man's throat. He didn't move. She picked up the gun, then nudged the man's head with her foot. He didn't respond, but Michael did. She heard a pathetic whimper and a low, feeble growl.

Melissa gently touched Michael's neck and spoke to him softly. The dog pulled himself away from the unconscious man and into Melissa's arms. That's when she felt the wet, sticky fur across his chest.

"Good boy, Michael," she whispered. "You saved me twice tonight."

It was at that moment that she thought she heard a faint whisper behind her. "Good dog." Startled, she looked over her shoulder, but the doorway was empty.

"Stay away from me," a voice stammered from the living room. It sounded like Mitch.

Gently moving Michael from her lap, Melissa picked up the gun and dropped it into the pocket of her pajamas. She retrieved the sword and stepped to the doorway. Mitch was walking backward, his eyes wide and his hands still tied behind his back. When the wall separating the living room from the kitchen stopped his retreat, he pressed his body against it, like he was trying to push himself through the wall and into the next room.

A tall, burley man, dressed like a fisherman, was holding a transparent filet knife inches from the terrified burglar's throat. The fisherman looked exactly like the man in the portrait. She watched, mesmerized, as the intruder's eyes rolled back in his head and he passed out cold, sliding down the wall to the floor. When Mitch dropped to the floor, Bernard's image dissolved.

"Bernard," Melissa called out, forced to acknowledge Bernard's existence as readily as she accepted his help.

She returned to the kitchen. Melissa put the sword on the table. She telephoned the police and an ambulance, then called the emergency veterinary clinic. Michael's breathing was shallow but steady. Though he wasn't bleeding heavily, Michael had been seriously injured. She put her hand on his shoulder and spoke to him softly while she waited for the police.

***

Melissa marveled at the skill of the veterinarian. Her expertise had saved Michael's life. Except for a pronounced limp, the dog had fully recovered. He still loved their walks and did not allow his injury to slow him down.

Melissa had not seen any apparitions in the house since the night of the break-in. Several times, however, she had seen a burley fisherman walking along the cliffs, with his arm around the shoulders of a lovely, dark-haired woman. A beautiful Newfoundland walked beside them.

The old black dog always woofed when the man raised his arm and waved to her. As Melissa waved back, the Bernard never failed to look at Michael and whisper, "Good dog."

###

One Step at a Time

Eli and his wife, Maria, made their home on the mountain, in the center of about one hundred and fifty acres of land that had been passed down for generations. They lived simply, hunted and fished in season, and gardened in the summer. Maria was an expert at canning, smoking and drying food, and they had a large root cellar where she could store fresh vegetables for months without spoiling. With the convenience of the internet and satellite service that worked more often than not, Eli worked at home as an investment counselor. His skill in advising the clients he had accumulated over the years allowed him to earn all the money he and Maria needed to live quite comfortably.

Several weeks prior, Eli had noticed a prowler lurking outside his front window before sunrise. He spotted the furry shadow as it dashed into the forest and believed that his intruder was likely a bear that had seen him, too, and was frightened away. Eli was fine with the idea that his face proved so frightful to the bear. As long as the critters didn't cause any damage, Eli was comfortable with the beasts that shared his territory, and there were many.

Eli returned to his father's old hickory rocker, and warmed by the crackling fire, he listened to the ticking of his mother's antique clock, which rested on the mantel above the fireplace. Again, he thought of his son, Paul, who had passed away fourteen years ago in a cabin fire just over the ridge from Eli and Maria's log home. The remains of Eli's two-year-old grandson, Gordon, were never found. The authorities said the fire could have consumed them, but Eli knew it was more than likely that the toddler's remains had been dragged away by coyotes. Paul's body was recovered fifty feet from the burning structure, still clutching Gordon's blanket. Paul's wife, Camille, had survived the fire, but the heat and the smoke had damaged her lungs. She lived with Eli and Maria for a couple of years following the tragedy, but had succumbed to lung disease, coupled with a broken heart.

Maria was in Louisiana. She was staying with her sister for a couple of weeks, so Eli didn't need to worry about disturbing her if he prowled around the cabin all night. He decided to stay up and watch for his visitor. Eli pulled the rocker a few feet away from its spot by the fireplace, where he'd have a clear view of the window. He tuned the radio to a classical music station, rocked in his chair, and watched. Three hours later, he was rewarded by the stalker's return.

Eli was at first startled, but then entranced by the figure, who seemed to materialize from the edge of the forest, before moving warily from the thick vegetation to the edge of the field yet staying in the shadows. The creature paused, surveyed the area, and then loped toward the cabin. Eli's eyesight was not what it once was, but he didn't think he was watching a bear.

Hidden behind the curtains, Eli sat motionless and silently observed as the figure moved to the side of the cabin just outside the window. As he watched, willing the creature to move to the front of the glass, Eli thought back to another day over forty years ago.

He and his father had been hunting elk, hoping to secure meat for the winter. Eli's father had circled around behind his son, trying to herd the elk toward Eli and into the sights of his rifle. Eli vividly remembered the fur covered beast that dashed from the trees directly toward him. He raised his rifle and was ready to fire but didn't pull the trigger. It wasn't an elk, nor was it a bear that he saw. The being that loped toward him was fur-covered but jogged on two legs. Astonished at the sight, Eli had remained frozen in place, opting not to shoot unless an attack was eminent. The beast was only ten yards away before it saw him and came to a halt. Eli lowered his rifle and locked eyes with what he immediately recognized as the mysterious Sasquatch. Neither of them moved for what seemed like an eternity. Then Eli smiled and slowly nodded. The creature tilted its head to the side, took two steps backward, pivoted, and disappeared into the woods. Seconds later, Eli's father walked out from the trees, close to the place from where the creature had emerged.

"Did you see him?" Eli stammered.

"I did," his father had replied. "We don't see the Sasquatch often, because they usually see us first. I'm certain that they watch us. Some people call them Bigfoot. They live deep in the mountains and have been here for centuries. From what I've seen, they are gentle beings, but they need protection from hunters and tourists. We don't speak of their presence to outsiders. In fact, we deny their existence."

"I really saw a Bigfoot," Eli said.

With a smile, his father replied, "Yes, you really did. Your grandfather and your great-grandfather saw them, too, and many ancestors before them. The sightings have become much less frequent, though, as their territory has been diminished. The Sasquatch clans travel the mountain ranges. Occasionally, one will walk too close to a road or might be surprised by people they aren't expecting to see in the area. If someone sees a Sasquatch, however, it's usually a young and inexperienced one. They are experts in stealth and camouflage. If you're ever asked about the Bigfoot, or if someone claims they've seen one, it's best to reply that it was likely a bear. The ancient creatures can use a little bit of help now and again, especially if they are to continue to survive. Our family has tried to provide that help for generations."

Father and son's experience that day remained a secret within their family. Throughout the years after, Eli occasionally found tracks he was certain were made by a Sasquatch. On two occasions, he'd seen what he was sure had been a spot where a Sasquatch bedded down in a storm. While Eli had never stopped hoping for another encounter, he had not seen another one of the elusive creatures since that day with his father.

Snow flurries started to obscure Eli's view through the glass, and as the clock chimed twice, he saw the voyeur cross in front of the window before disappearing into the night. For a minute more, Eli sat quietly, scarcely daring to breathe. He had seen his nighttime stalker, and it was clearly running on two legs.

***

Dawn was breaking. Still thinking of the creature he'd seen in the early morning hours, Eli briskly made his way through the pristine, snow-covered path toward the river. Carrying his fishing pole and an auger to break through the ice, he was looking forward to a fish dinner. Close to the water's edge, he slowed his pace and walked carefully toward the center of the ice-covered river. The ice was thick, so he had no concern that it would crack beneath his weight.

After using the auger to break through the ice, Eli chipped away at the frozen edges of the fishing hole. He was expanding the rough circle, so he could better see where the deeper water was running when he lost his footing. A bellow involuntarily escaped his lips as he slid into the freezing abyss. He spread his arms across the ice, on either side of the hole, just in time to keep his head and shoulders above the water.

Frantically treading water, while trying to keep his arms stretched across the top of the slippery ice, Eli knew he would freeze to death in a matter of minutes if he didn't get out. If he placed his forearms on the ice and held them steady, he hoped his jacket would freeze to the surface, so that he could get leverage to raise his legs and get his feet up onto the ledge surrounding him. Steadily kicking his legs in a scissors motion, Eli planted his forearms on the ice.

Eli's legs and feet were numb, and he was losing the feeling in his hands. Fighting the desire to close his eyes and submit to the darkness that threatened death, Eli struggled to keep his head above the water. Exhaustion was taking over. He felt himself sliding below the surface of the river just before someone pulled him from the water and onto the ice.

***

Eli drifted in and out of consciousness. He remembered being dragged from the river, freezing and trembling. Now, wrapped in blankets and shivering violently, he heard the crackling of a fire. He was inside a structure, stretched out on the floor in front of a fireplace. He wondered who brought him to safety. As he struggled to open his eyes, his mind relayed more bits and pieces to his memory. Or, he wondered, had it all been a dream?

Eli was, however, certain that he had never felt so cold. He knew he had been dragged from the water, his limp body lifted, then carried, apparently for some distance. The only neighbor within over a mile was Caleb Handler. Eli supposed Caleb might have gone to the river to fish. Maybe Caleb was behind him and had gotten to the river in time to pull him from the water, but Eli didn't remember hearing Caleb's voice. Although his neighbor was small in stature, he might have dragged Eli from the ice. Caleb could not have carried him any distance, however, and he surely would have spoken to Eli.

Eli recalled branches brushing against his back and his legs. He heard the crunch of snow and heavy breathing that was not his own. He also thought he felt fur rubbing against his face as he bounced through the woods at what he felt was a not quite human pace.

Could it be? He wondered. Would he open his eyes to see a face surrounded by the dark fur of a Sasquatch? Would a Bigfoot understand enough to wrap a freezing man in blankets, or add wood to a fire?

When he opened his eyes, the first thing he saw was his own fireplace and the old clock on the mantel. At the squeak of floorboards, Eli turned his head and looked into oddly familiar eyes. As blackness descended again, he wondered how it was possible.

***

Gor added wood to the smoldering logs in the hearth. He had carried the man to the cabin and wrapped him in as many blankets as he could quickly find. The heat from the fireplace was warming the cabin, and the old man's shakes had nearly quelled. Gor knew that was good.

Gor's mind was at work, prodded when he'd locked eyes with those of the old man, trying to coax some long-ago memory forward. Sitting on the floor of the cabin, watching the fire, the fog of the past grew clearer, details emerging.

Very young…strange sounds…frightened…. flashes of fiery orange…eyes burn…fingers hurt…hard to breathe…powerful arms…

Gordon remembered the muscular arms that had picked him up, carried him into the frosty night air, spilled him into the snow, then reached again and pulled him close, providing warmth as the arms wrapped around him.

Protector's arms…Daddy's arms wrapping around me…

Gordon had slept.

Cold…hungry…powerful arms…

He remembered being lifted again. The arms, muscular and firm, which pressed him against soft, thick fur, carried him from the cold ground to a warm, safe place.

Gordon had lived with the clan in the mountains ever since. Their vocalizations were primitive, but through their gestures, they could communicate until he learned their language. They called him *Gor*, a shortened version of the name he had repeated to them. They raised him as one of their own.

He grew, knowing he was different from the rest of his clan, but until the present moment, he hadn't realized that he belonged to the tribe of man.

***

When Eli awoke again, his shivering had subsided. He gathered the blankets around his shoulders and pushed himself up to a sitting position. He thought he was alone until he tried to stand and firm hands materialized to steady him as his knees threatened to fail him.

"Thank you," Eli murmured, as he turned and stared at the young man, who had backed away as soon as Eli was on his feet. At first, this young man appeared to be the image of Paul. He had the same dark hair and the sun-darkened skin of an outdoorsman, but with a beard that covered most of his face. He wore a knee-length tunic made from what looked like a bearskin.

Without turning his eyes away from his rescuer, Eli slid a wooden stool close to the fireplace. The wild-looking man was taller than Paul, who would logically be much older than the man Eli was watching. But if Eli's grandson, Gordon, had lived, he would have been about the age of the young man sitting on the floor. Eli wondered if it was possible.

His father's words echoed in Eli's psyche: *"We don't see the Sasquatch often, but they watch us."*

Eli, his hand quivering slightly, carefully reached toward the young man and asked, "Is your name Gordon?"

At the sound of his name, the young man jerked back, as though pushed. He didn't respond, but kept his eyes locked with Eli's.

"I won't do anything to hurt you," Eli murmured, slowly standing. He wanted to touch Gordon, although Eli had feared that his motion would send this young mountain man running in fright.

Wary, moving away from Eli's reach, Gor took a step backward, never looking away from the older man.

Eli turned his hand palm up and curled his fingers, motioning his rescuer to move nearer. "Please, come closer," he whispered.

Though doubtful that his words would be understood, Eli was confident his gestures would suffice. A minute passed while the two men simply studied each other. Their conversation was poignant, though neither uttered a word, until the younger man touched his own chest and said, "Gor."

"Gor?" Eli repeated. His hand trembled as he reached to touch his rescuer. "Gor-don, Gor-don?" He pronounced as he pleaded for confirmation. It finally came as he caressed the mountain man's misshapen fingers and discovered the scarred tissue that began at Gordon's fingertips and disappeared into the sleeve of his tunic.

"I am your grandfather," Eli said.

Gor timidly extended his hand to brush Eli's cheek. "Gor-don," he said, nodding, his lips forming an uncertain smile.

Exhausted, Eli was also exhilarated. The old clock chimed, and he looked toward it. When he turned back, Gordon was gone. Through the window, Eli watched his grandson jog across the field of snow and dash into the forest.

Eli couldn't wait to tell Maria. He wanted to shout from the top of the mountain that he had found his grandson, but unless Gordon chose to move back to civilization, Eli realized he could tell no one that his grandson was alive. How could he explain the appearance of a sixteen-year-old man-child who had spent the last fourteen years living in the mountains of New York, with little human contact? If people heard the story, Bigfoot hunters would arrive en masse, some with cameras, but many with bullets. Campsites would litter the pristine mountainsides with no regard for private property or wildlife habitat, disrupting the tranquility of the mountain, possibly for years to come. He could tell only Maria, but not yet.

The sun would set soon. Eli locked the cabin door, as was his habit after dark. He stacked a couple more logs on the fire, then undressed and took a lengthy hot shower. After dressing in long underwear and flannel pajamas, he heated a can of vegetable soup for dinner. He ate quickly, then went to bed. There would be no vigil that night. Eli was exhausted.

"One step at a time," Eli whispered to the cabin walls, just before drifting off into a dreamless sleep. He knew it wouldn't be long before Gordon returned, and he had to figure out how to make him want to stay.

###

A Candle in the Darkness

Flashing and dancing, lightning illuminated the sky like fireworks on the fourth of July. A brilliant display of nature's power, the light show's beauty was lost in the violence of the storm. Bursts of lightning in the moonless sky coincided with the whistle of the airstream gusts that roared past the windshield as they slammed into the side of the car. The car shuddered and swayed, and as Valerie fought to maintain control, she wondered if the wind could be strong enough to blow her car into the ditch at the edge of the roadway.

Her husband's funeral had been that morning. Valerie replayed the afternoon in her mind, teeth clenched, as her white knuckles gripped the steering wheel.

"Listen, Valerie," his mother said, as they lowered Randy's coffin into the ground. "You'll hear him whisper, almost as if it's a dream. He's just away. Randy will never leave us."

Valerie didn't hear a thing.

Randy is gone, she thought. *He died, and the dead don't come back. Dead husbands don't watch over you and they don't protect you. They get buried in the ground.*

Friends and family gathered at her in-laws' house after the funeral. Valerie couldn't wait to escape the endless condolences, the stories of Randy's childhood, the promises that everything would work out, and most of all, Randy's mother's insistence that he was still with them. Valerie needed to go home, even though home was a twelve-hour drive east.

"But Valerie," her mother-in-law said, "bad weather is forecast. You don't want to get caught in a storm. At least stay until tomorrow."

"Weather forecasts are wrong more often than they're right," Valerie had replied. "I need to get home and the quicker I hit the road, the sooner I'll get there."

Her mother-in-law meant well, but Valerie couldn't stay in that house another hour.

Her mind wandered. She recalled the day he died. Randy

was on his way home. His plane crashed on take-off. It was a freak accident that killed Randy and three others. The Army sent their condolences. Randy came home a day later. They carried him off the plane in a wooden box, covered by an American Flag. She didn't know how she could go on without him in her life.

Driving through the rain with tears streaming down her face, Valerie would never touch his face or hear his voice again. She would never hold his hand or feel the comfortable protection of his arm draped across her shoulder.

There was minimal traffic on the road. She hadn't seen another car for quite a few miles. Occasional static interrupted the soft jazz station on the radio, but it startled her when the emergency beeping sounded. A mechanical voice interrupted the music, "This is an announcement from the emergency broadcasting system. A tornado watch has been issued for the general area surrounding Ralston, in Tyrone County."

Great, she thought, trying to visualize the map to get an idea about where she was. *I can't be too far from Ralston. With my luck, I'm right in the middle of Tyrone County.*

It was close to midnight, but Valerie had hoped to get to Ralston and find a room for the night. The storm was increasing in strength. It was difficult and it became almost impossible to see the road ahead. She slowed the car to a crawl and was looking for a place to pull off the road to check the map and wait out the storm when she saw a light blinking ahead.

Relieved, she continued her slow-motion drive toward the light that cut through the rain and fog. Grateful for good luck, she turned into a small, empty parking lot under a blinking billboard that flashed the letters: VACANCY. She was at the Traveler's Rest Motel. Valerie pulled the car to the front of the motel lobby and parked as close to the door as she was able.

With the rain blowing sideways, there was no sense in even trying to use an umbrella, and so she dashed from the car to the lobby. Her sneakers made a squishing noise and drops of rain fell from her long, dark hair as she crossed the vinyl floor to the front desk. She pushed the top of a little silver bell that sat on the corner of the desk. The lobby was quiet, with no sign of any other guests. After a minute, when she still heard nothing, Valerie touched the bell again.

"Hello? Is anyone around?" There was no response.

She turned to go back to her car but hesitated. If a tornado was going to hit anywhere close, she would be better off inside a building than inside her car. She was watching the storm and didn't hear the night clerk approach.

"Hello there," she said. "Are you looking for a room for the night?"

"Oh, hi. I didn't hear you come in. The storm is making it impossible to drive, and I heard an announcement about a tornado watch. When I saw your vacancy sign, I thought it would be better to stop here than to stay on the road. I suspect anyone else driving out there will do the same thing."

The woman smiled, "Welcome to Traveler's Rest. My name is Dorene. I'll get you checked in right away. The storm is looking fierce. Will you need a room for two?"

"No," Valerie answered. "It's just me." *From now on,* she thought, *it's always going to be just me.*

Dorene smiled and nodded, then pulled open a drawer and lifted out an oversized ledger. "It's good that you stopped. You wouldn't want to be driving if a twister comes through. We had one hit here about 40 years ago. It destroyed Traveler's Rest. We had a nice little town here, back then. Nasty things those tornadoes are. Sign here and you'll be all set."

Valerie signed her name on the ledger and gave Dorene her credit card. The clerk took the card and copied the numbers onto a tablet.

"If this storm gets any worse, you'd best move to the cellar out back." Dorene held out the key. "You're in room five." She reached under the counter and brought up a candle. Melted wax stuck the partially burned candle to the bottom of an old mason jar.

"Take this with you in case we lose electric power. If the lights go out, you'll need a candle in the darkness." She gave Valerie the candle and a packet of matches.

"You can leave your car where it is and walk through the breezeway to room 5. You'll pass the stairs to the cellar on your way to your room. They are on the right side of the breezeway."

"If you need to get to the cellar, be sure to bring your candle. There's no light down there."

"Thank you, Dorene. Let's hope the tornado misses us."

The rain was pouring off the roof like a giant waterfall. Valerie was going to get soaked if she went back to her car, but she wanted the little flashlight that was in the glove compartment and her tote bag. Her book, a sweater, a bottle of water and a couple of granola bars were stashed in that bag. She had a suitcase in the trunk, but the tote bag was all she'd need to get through the night.

Valerie dashed to her car, retrieved her tote and tossed her purse, flashlight, and the candle into the bag. She locked the car, trotted back through the rain to the motel, then walked, shivering and with her shoes still squishing, through the breezeway in search of room number five.

The lightning continued, and the rain wasn't letting up. The wind rattled the windows and pounded the rain into the walls of the building. Valerie opened the door to room five, turned on the lights, and locked the door behind her. The tops of the old furniture glistened and smelled of lemon, as if recently polished. Dust-free, ivory-colored lampshades covered the dim lightbulbs on a pair of brass lamps that lit the room. The orange carpet was worn, but spotless, and the bed was covered with a bright orange and green chenille bedspread. There was a blanket at the foot of the bed. An old-fashioned clock-radio sat on a small stand next to a little square ashtray that held a pack of matches.

Valerie set her bag on the bed, found the candle, lit it and set it next to the ashtray. *Atmosphere,* she thought. Randy had always liked candlelight and would have loved the old-fashioned motel room.

She walked into the bathroom and dried some rain with one of the clean white towels. Her reflection in the spotless mirror showed mascara running down her cheeks like black tears. It wasn't a good idea to take a shower in a storm, but she figured washing her face would be okay. As she was rinsing the soap from her cheeks, she heard Dorene knocking on the door.

"Valerie," Dorene called, "a tornado is coming. We need to go to the cellar now." The knocking became more insistent. The room was vibrating with the innkeeper's pounding.

Valerie pulled a clean white towel from the rack, scrubbed it across her face, and hollered back to Dorene, "Thank you, I'm coming."

The lights went out.

The canning jar candle provided enough light to guide her to the door.

She picked up her tote bag, threw it over her shoulder, grabbed the candle, and hurried across the room.

Dorene was pacing outside the door. “Quickly! I can hear it coming.”

Valerie had once been told that a tornado sounded like a train and the sound of a freight train surrounded her. It hadn’t been Dorene’s pounding that caused her room to vibrate. It was the atmosphere that carried the tornado, and it was almost on top of them.

“Follow me,” Dorene hollered above the noise. “We have to hurry.”

Dorene held a lantern in front of her and turned toward the breezeway. The wind was howling and rain was blowing through the tunnel like a giant fire hose, threatening to push them off their feet as they made their way toward the cellar. Cold and shivering, Valerie looked forward to pulling on her sweater. She wished she had thought of taking the blanket from the bed.

Valerie followed closely behind Dorene, her flickering candle providing some comfort, but not as much light as Dorene’s lantern. It was a short distance from her room to the cellar, but the conditions made it seem like a marathon. Still, they managed to make their way down the slippery, wet stairs to the cellar door.

Dorene opened the door to the underground room and held the lantern up so Valerie could see as they entered the small enclosure. The cellar was small and completely underground. The dirt floor was packed solid, and a large portion was covered with flagstone. Wooden shelves were mounted on two sides of the cellar. The shelves were filled with mason jars of fruits and vegetables and several dark glass bottles, which could have been wine, beer, root beer, or a combination of the three. There was a wooden bench on the back wall. Even through the heavy wooden door, they could hear the wind roaring.

“You’ll be fine here.” Dorene smiled at Valerie. “A lot of people have weathered a lot of storms down in this old cellar. It’s a safe place.”

Valerie set her candle on the shelf and slipped into her sweater. She took the flashlight from the tote, turned it on, and said, "This might help a light the cellar a little more." The small flashlight brightened, then flickered and went out.

"Oh, no," Valerie said. "I just put new batteries in this. I can't believe they died." She turned it off, then on again. There was nothing.

Dorene said, "There should be some more candles down here. Look on that second shelf, near the carrots."

Valerie shuffled a few jars and reached for two mason jars. Each held a tapered candle stuck to the bottom with melted wax, just like the one Dorene had given her.

Valerie lit the candles, and Dorene said, "I used to help my mom can food from the garden in the back of the motel. I always liked to see the jars lined up on the shelves."

Dorene gestured toward one of the small dark brown bottles on the shelf and said, "There should be a bottle opener nailed on the end of the shelf by the door. Open a bottle of root beer and try it."

Sure enough, there was a metal bottle opener nailed to the edge of one of the shelves. Valerie slid the root beer bottle under the opener, popped off the top and took a small sip of the dark brown liquid.

"This is wonderful," Valerie responded. Despite the situation and her frame of mind, the drink lifted her spirits. "It's the best root beer I've ever tasted."

"My uncle used to make the best root beer. He let it age, sometimes for years. He would be pleased to have another root beer fan," Dorene told her.

"I'm surprised you don't have a lot more business tonight," Valerie said. "There wasn't much traffic, but I figured anyone who was driving through would stop when they saw your lights. Of course, now there are no lights, so I guess no one else will be coming in."

The two women walked over to the bench and sat down to wait out the storm. With the candles lit and the oil lantern burning, there was enough light to allow them to look around the small cave. Flickering flames cast shadows that gave the illusion of dancers behind the shelves. It was cool and damp in their refuge, but they were dry and out of danger and they sat together quietly like old friends.

"The last tornado to come through Traveler's Rest was in 1972. The motel was about half full of tourists. Most were families, some with young children. Back then, there wasn't much of a notification process in place. We get lots of storms this time of year, and that day we knew it was a storm that was different from most. Stephen and I got everybody to the cellar, though. When the tornado hit, it came through fast and it was violent. It was just so sudden. The roof fell first and then the walls collapsed. The noise was terrible. It was loud and black as a moonless night. Then, as suddenly as it hit, there was silence. People were packed in this little cellar pretty tight, but they got through the storm in one piece."

Dorene stopped talking and looked up, as the cellar door opened and a bearded, gray-haired man came in. He ushered a young couple in front of him.

"Dorene," the man said. "I've made it home. I guess you were expecting me."

"Yes, Stephen. I have been waiting for you," the innkeeper replied.

Her blue eyes sparkled in the candlelight, and she showed off her white teeth with a smile that brightened her entire face. Dorene wrapped her arms around the big man's neck and he lifted her off the ground with a bear hug and a grin.

"It's good to have you back," she said. "Who are your friends?"

"I found these two in the parking lot and thought I'd better get them to the cellar. I didn't take time for introductions, though." Stephen replied. "I figured I'd find you here. It's bad out there."

The young man spoke, "I'm Grant Myers, and this is my wife, Felicia. We sure do appreciate you allowing us to join you down here. We almost missed the motel in the dark, but Felicia saw your lantern and we pulled into the parking lot to get off the road. I guess you heard there's a tornado warning. The weather service radar spotted a funnel cloud, moving toward Ralston."

Stephen said, "That isn't good news. Ralston is only four miles down the road." Stephen continued. "This feels just like the storm back in seventy-two."

Turning to Grant and Felicia, Stephen said, "We might be here for a little while. It was good luck that you had those sleeping bags. They'll be more comfortable to sit on than the stone floor."

Felicia said, "Thank you so much for getting us out of the storm. If you have a room available, we'd like to spend the night once the threat is past."

The cellar door shuddered and there was a roar like a freight train rolling down the cellar steps, ready to crash through the heavy old wooden door.

Stephen pointed to a flat-sided log on top of some planks stacked under the shelves. "Grant, would you grab that log and put it up here on these braces for me?"

"Sure," Grant replied. He immediately picked up the log and settled it on the rusted metal brackets attached to the wall on either side of the door.

"Thanks," Stephen told him. "My back isn't what it used to be. That will hold the door closed, just in case that old latch wants to give way."

Suddenly, there was silence.

"Listen," Valerie said. "It's quiet." She stood up.

Dorene said, "You might want to sit back down for a few minutes. I think the worst is yet to come."

Stephen walked over to the bench, sat next to Dorene, and put his arm around her shoulders. Grant and Felicia wrapped the sleeping bags around themselves and sat on the floor, leaning back against the wall.

The roaring of the wind began again. It pounded on the cellar door, and Valerie was glad that Grant had put the wooden log across the inside. There was a loud thud, then another. The door shook but stayed closed.

Felicia buried her face in Grant's shoulder. Stephen pulled Dorene a little closer, and Valerie hugged her sweater around her chest. No one spoke.

The noise intensified, then gradually quieted, until the only sound was the breathing of five people locked in the musty, old cellar. Exhausted, Valerie closed her eyes and embraced the comforting oblivion of sleeping on the ancient wooden bench.

Valerie woke to voices. Grant and Felicia had slept on the ground. Grant was stretching as Felicia peeled the sleeping bag off.

"Good morning," Felicia said, when she saw Valerie was awake. "I didn't hear Stephen and Dorene leave, but they're gone.

The storm must be over. I wonder how long we've been sleeping."

"I didn't hear them either," Grant responded. "They probably went to check on the damage. I can't believe we fell asleep. I'll go out and see if the motel is still standing." He crossed the small space, lifted the log brace from the wall, and opened the door.

They looked up the steps and squinted at the brightness of the morning. They could see that the rain had stopped. A steady wind was still blowing, but after what they had experienced the night before, it was like a soft breeze.

"My goodness," Valerie whispered, "we slept all night."

Debris was piled at the bottom of the stairs. "We're lucky the whole stairway didn't fill with rubble," Grant exclaimed, moving a wooden plank, a few bricks and a concrete block to allow them access to the steps.

Grant went up the steps first, with Felicia right behind him and Valerie bringing up the rear. At the top of the stairs, they froze. Traveler's Rest Motel had been destroyed. There were a few rooms standing, one of which was room five, where Valerie had been the night before. Part of the lobby remained intact. The roof was missing, but two walls stood and protected the front desk from the wind. The vacancy sign was still hanging, though only by one old and rusted chain.

Valerie's car had been moved to the far end of the parking lot, but except for the wooden door that covered the trunk and part of the back windshield, the car appeared to be undamaged. Grant and Felicia's car was in front of the lobby where they had left it, but the storm had rolled it over onto the driver's side, with the four wheels facing west.

"It looks like my car survived with minimal damage. If it will start, I can give you a ride into town."

"We'd appreciate that," Grant said. "I'm going to take a walk over to what's left of the lobby and try to find Stephen and Dorene."

Valerie and Felicia went back to the cellar to get their things, while Grant searched for the others.

"No sign of them," Grant said.

"How strange that they would just leave us," Valerie told them. "Although I can only imagine their shock when they saw

Dorene's Motel, her home, gone."

Grant removed the door from the back of Valerie's car. The corner of the back windshield was cracked, but otherwise intact. They got into the car, and Valerie was rewarded with the familiar roar of the engine when she turned the key. The trio headed toward Ralston.

Only four miles into town, the drive took close to an hour. Uprooted trees and piles of debris littered the roadway. There was no traffic. Valerie alternated between the oncoming and outgoing lanes to avoid the blockages. Twice, she had to stop the car so they could get out to move large branches in order to continue on the highway.

Ralston had some damage, but most of the buildings remained standing. They saw a sign, *Max's Garage*, above a building that was pretty much undamaged. There was an old man sitting on the bench in front of the office. Valerie pulled the car up near the bench and Grant got out.

"Is there any chance somebody is available to tow a car to Ralston, from the Traveler's Rest Motel?" Grant asked.

The old man said, "My son runs this place now. He's out with the truck. I guess he'll be back in an hour or so. You're welcome to wait here, or there's a café down the block that has clean water. They have coffee and they're cooking eggs and toast, if you're hungry." The man stood and held out his right hand. "I'm Max."

Grant shook Max's hand and replied, "Nice to meet you, Max. My name is Grant. This is my bride, Felicia, and our friend, Valerie."

"You say your car is at the Traveler's Rest Motel?" the old man asked.

"Yes," Grant replied. "We pulled off the road just before the tornado hit. Thank heaven, a man saw us in the parking lot and took us to the motel's cellar. He said his name was Stephen. I didn't get his last name."

"Stephen?" the old man repeated with a slow smile.

"Yes." Grant told him. "He and the owner of the motel, Dorene, barricaded themselves in the cellar with us. They likely saved our lives. We all fell asleep waiting out the storm, but when we woke up this morning, Stephen and Dorene were already gone.

The motel was demolished."

"Fischer." Max said. "His last name is Fischer. Stephen and Dorene Fischer ran Traveler's Rest Motel until a tornado destroyed it back in the seventies."

"That must have been Dorene's parents," Valerie said, nodding her head. "Dorene mentioned the tornado that hit Traveler's Rest in the seventies. How sad to lose a home twice." She sighed.

"Stephen and Dorene didn't have any children." Max told them. "They lived there at the motel with Dorene's parents until the tornado. That tornado went right through Traveler's Rest. It demolished the motel alright, and the little village that surrounded it was leveled, too. But almost everyone who was there that day survived."

Valerie, Grant, and Felicia looked at each other silently as the old man continued with his story.

"During the storm, Dorene's parents were in the cellar, along with about a dozen and a half people who had been guests at the motel, and the few shop owners who lived in Travelers Rest. They were packed in that little cellar like sardines, but nobody got hurt." Max shook his head. "Stephen and Dorene got all the motel guests to the cellar, along with the few residents of Traveler's Rest. The tornado hit before they could get underground themselves."

Grant interrupted, "The brace was up against the door. I put the log across the cellar door when we came in last night," he explained. "I remember thinking that nothing was going to get through the door with that log across it. How did Stephen and Dorene get out if the log was still across the door, from the inside?"

"Oh Grant, there must be another entrance to the cellar." Felicia told him, chuckling. "It's an old motel and an old cellar. A lot of places had tunnels back then." She turned to Max. "You were saying that Stephen and Dorene didn't get to the cellar when the tornado came through. What happened to them?"

The old man took a deep breath and told them, "Stephen and Dorene were together in the breezeway when the tornado hit. Dorene was killed when one of the concrete walls collapsed on her. Stephen was hurt pretty badly. He stayed in a coma for a week, as I recall, but he survived. After he recovered, Stephen came back to

Ralston. He stayed here, in Ralston, for the rest of his life."

Grant spoke first. "So, it was Stephen who helped us last night. What a coincidence that the woman with him was also named Dorene."

The old man smiled. "It was no coincidence. Dorene died that night, but she never left Traveler's Rest. Her spirit has been a candle in the darkness for more than one traveler out on that lonely road."

Max chuckled. "As for Stephen, it looks like he's back with Dorene for good. Stephen passed away yesterday afternoon."

The dread that surrounded her since Randy's death felt like a lead cape weighing her down. In that moment, the cape was lifted from her shoulders, replaced by the familiar comfort of Randy's arm, slung casually across her back, and she remembered Randy's much-repeated promise, "I'll love you forever."

The old man must have noticed something, too, because he looked directly into her eyes and said, "People die. That's for sure. But every so often, if they have reason enough, they come back for a while. Some even stay right here with us. Now and again, they let us know they're around, but we won't ever hear them, if we don't listen, and we won't ever see them, if we don't believe."

"I believe," Valerie murmured, and then, almost like a dream, she heard a whisper, "Well, it's about time."

Unintended Consequences

The solid slam of the steel door convinced me that, until that moment, I had under-appreciated the concept of liberty. My expectation of an abysmal future was reinforced by the clunk of locks engaged behind me. Even if I could flee captors who flanked me on the walk to my cell, there was no exit from this hellhole. I had arrived at my new home as a consequence of my actions yet wondered if my fate was truly justice.

My imagination was making a desperate attempt to reinvent my surroundings. I wanted to envision my little patio, a cacophony of herbs there to greet me every day with the blended fragrance of lavender and rosemary. I found the memory, but the image quickly faded against the rancid odor of disinfectant spread with filthy mops. I wondered if I would ever smell lavender again. My psyche was screaming, telling me to drop to the floor and close my eyes until the nightmare ended. Would I ever again awaken in my bedroom, with sunlight streaming through the windows? Would I ever hold Anita again? Would Frank ever forgive me?

I wanted to turn and run, but what little fortitude I had remaining caused me to fixate on moving one foot in front of the other lest my legs refuse to walk.

Sobs ricocheted off the block partitions, coupled with obscenities thrown like spears across the walkway. I tried to recall the lyrics to some of my favorite songs, but the words hovered just out of reach. Instead of the verse I was so desperately trying to recollect, I heard one of my escorts order, "Halt."

I raised my eyes to an opening in the bars that formed in front of one of the many block and mortar compartments lining the walls. Yet, before entering the dim and gloomy cave, I had to shut my eyes again to prevent the tears from exposing my despair. I heard the slam of the steel bars behind me, but kept my eyes closed until the footsteps of the guards retreated into oblivion.

I thought back to the night it happened.

Frank hadn't expected me home until ten-thirty that

evening. It was nine o'clock when I walked through the door. I heard Anita whimper before I saw her bent over the sofa. Frank was standing behind her, wearing only his boxer shorts. His hands were pressed into Anita's waist, and he was pulling our eleven-year-old daughter toward him.

Anita's softball bat was leaning against the wall and I grabbed it. Gripping the bat with both hands, I swung with all my strength, connecting with Frank's right temple. He dropped to the floor.

Anita whimpered again. Her eyes were wide with terror as tears ran down her cheeks. She turned toward me, wheezed, and grabbed her throat. It was then that I understood she was choking. I pushed her over the sofa and wrapped both arms around her diaphragm. Now I understood what Frank was doing when I walked into the room. I pulled backward once, then twice, before successfully dislodging the kernel of popcorn that had been blocking Anita's trachea.

She gasped and then shakily exhaled before she saw the blood flowing from her father's skull, as he lay deathly still.

"Daddy," she screamed.

Dropping to my knees, I felt Frank's neck and then his wrist, praying for a pulse. There was none. I turned him over onto his back, put my ear to his chest and listened for the familiar sound of his heart beating. How many times had I fallen asleep to that sound? I couldn't count them. This time, there was no sound. I attempted CPR, knowing the effort was futile, but I kept trying. There was no response. Finally, I admitted Frank was gone.

"Anita," I calmly said as I stood and pulled her tight against me, turning her away from the grisly scene at her feet, "Daddy fell and hit his head. I have to help him, so I need you to go upstairs to your room and pack your suitcase. Put underwear, pajamas, and three of your favorite outfits into the suitcase. Aunt Monica is going to take you and Misha to her house for the weekend."

Misha was my daughter's confidant, a Siamese cat who rarely left her side. Not letting Anita look back, I escorted the confused child to the foot of the stairs. I needed to protect our daughter the best way I could. There was time to fall apart later.

"Hurry," I told her. "I'll call Aunt Monica and she'll be here in a minute."

Trusting her mother, Anita smiled bravely and ran up the stairs to gather her belongings.

I called Monica, told her I had an emergency and would explain later. I said that she needed to come for Anita. Monica loves Anita, and I knew she would care for her. It was important that Anita would be taken away from the sight of her father's murder as soon as possible. It was also important that she not see her mother dragged away in handcuffs. Monica didn't ask questions, instead left her home at once, and drove to pick up her niece.

I retrieved the cat carrier from the closet and called Misha, who quickly responded. As I stroked her beautiful mink-like coat, I asked her to take care of Anita, then placed her inside of the carrier to await my sister's arrival.

Our home had now become a crime scene. I went upstairs to help my eleven-year-old pack her clothes for the upcoming days. It was unlikely that Monica would be able to re-enter for several days, but I wanted Anita to have her clothes and some familiar possessions. The last thing I placed in her satchel was a picture of the three of us: Frank, Anita, and me. It had been taken at the county fair just the week before. We were happy and laughing. Last week, our lives were perfect.

"Anita," I began, "Daddy is hurt and the ambulance will be here soon. I need to go with them. Aunt Monica will be here in a few minutes, and she'll take care of you until I can come back home."

"Will Daddy be okay?" Anita was trembling, confused and frightened.

"I'm sure the hospital will do everything they can to help him get better." There was no good reason to tell her, at that moment, that her father was dead, his skull crushed by her mother.

Monica arrived within fifteen minutes of my call. She burst through the front door. "Melanie," she called. "Are you okay? What …" The silence that followed told me she had seen Frank.

"We're on our way downstairs," I answered brightly, fighting tears, as I picked up Anita's suitcase and wondered how long it would be before I could see my daughter again.

"Anita's suitcase is all packed. She's ready for a vacation at your house, while I stay with Daddy and help him get better." I smiled, trying to look confident that everything would be fine.

"I'll go say goodbye to Daddy." Anita started toward the living room.

"Daddy went up to bed while you were packing your clothes," I lied. "He fell asleep right away. We're waiting for the doctor to come now."

Monica clearly understood that the situation was dire. Somehow, she knew I was responsible for Frank's condition. Not knowing if I planned to confess or to flee, she smiled at her niece and said, "This will be so much fun. I'm really excited to have you all to myself for a few days, Anita. I think tomorrow we can go to the zoo and then to the diner where they have those great French fries!"

Anita visibly relaxed. After all, if Aunt Monica was planning a day filled with fun, then everything must truly be alright. I kissed Anita and told her I'd see her soon. I hugged my sister and pressed my house keys and all the money that was in my wallet into her hand. She would need access to the house, and, where I was going, I wouldn't immediately need cash. As I watched my sister leave with my daughter, I called the police and told them I had just killed my husband.

The police arrived, along with the paramedics. There was nothing they could do for Frank, but I knew that. I was a doctor, sworn to first do no harm, yet I had killed the father of my child, the love of my life.

The police asked me question after question, but I couldn't seem to find the words to respond. I couldn't seem to find any words at all, as tears streamed silently down my cheeks.

I was handcuffed and ushered to the police car, where they carefully strapped me into the back seat. The drive to the police station seemed to take forever.

They read me my rights and asked if I wanted a lawyer. I didn't answer. I couldn't think, speak, or fully comprehend. A police officer escorted me to a small room, handcuffed my wrists and shackled my legs. There was a chair in the room. When I sat, the officer left me alone. I closed my eyes and prayed for God to take me right then. He didn't, and I started to scream.

Though Monica had come to the courthouse for the arraignment, I hadn't talked with her since the night of the murder.

I had neither seen nor spoken with Anita since that night, but I had written dozens of letters to her in my mind.

A judge asked, "How do you plead?"

I responded, "I killed Frank." After that, I had nothing else to say. Memories filled my mind. I remembered every detail of that night. I remembered the weight of the bat and the sickening crack when it collided with Frank's skull. I began hyperventilating, and then everything went black. They brought me here.

I was the newest resident of Mayville, the state hospital for the criminally insane.

Standing in the middle of my cell, I took inventory. I let myself cry and prayed that my heart would simply stop beating. I wondered if Frank was watching me. I wondered if he was waiting for me. Silently, I said the words I had been repeating constantly. *I'm so sorry, Frank. I'll always love you.*

I looked to my left and saw a concrete slab covered with a thin mattress. Sheets, a blanket and a pillow were stacked at the end of that slab, along with a roll of toilet paper, a bar of soap and a small stack of paper towels. A tiny rust-stained sink and a lidless toilet rounded out the décor. The depressing rectangle had no windows, and this new inmate, who treasured sunlight and fresh air, wasn't sure if she could survive a night, let alone years, in this cell.

My lawyer told me she couldn't help me if I didn't talk to her, but my mind was still in shock, so I couldn't speak. Maybe here, facing a lifetime of seclusion, I could form words that would not excuse, but would explain what I had done. If I told them exactly what happened, maybe there was a chance that I could someday go back to my life. Of course, it wouldn't really be my life without Frank.

Time held no meaning. It could have been minutes or hours after they locked me in the concrete closet that a woman approached. She had a cart filled with drinks. She stopped in front of my cell door.

"Hello, Melanie," she said. She was smiling and her eyes were kind and sympathetic. "Would you like something to drink? I have juice, ginger ale, and water."

I stood and walked to the cell door.

"How about some orange juice?" The woman suggested, as

she reached for a paper cup.

Nodding, I tried to smile, but the corners of my mouth refused to turn upward. She passed the cup of juice through the bars and into my hand. “My name is Linda. I work in the kitchen and usually bring the cart around for the people who aren’t up to spending time in the cafeteria. It’s nice to meet you, Melanie. I’ll see you again soon.”

I tasted the juice and was surprised at how wonderfully sweet it was. Fighting the urge to guzzle the drink, I sipped slowly, savoring every ounce. As I carried the cup to my cot, I realized how little I’d had to eat or drink. My mouth silently formed the words, “thank you.” Linda came to see me every day and though I didn’t speak to her, she understood we were friends.

The days became weeks, and the weeks morphed into months. Monica came to see me every Sunday. Today was Sunday. Monica would be here soon. There was so much I wanted to tell my sister, and so many questions I wanted to ask, but I couldn’t seem to find my voice. Every week, Monica told me what was going on in her life. She spoke about Anita and how she and Misha were inseparable. I always listened silently.

As usual, when friends and family arrived, I was escorted to the visitors’ lounge, where tables and chairs were placed throughout a large, tile floored room, with huge windows that allowed the light to shine in through the wire that was embedded in the glass. A psychiatric aide served as an overseer during visiting hours. They assigned Janet to the lounge today. Monica was already there when I arrived. Smiling her ever-ready smile, she stood when I walked in.

“How are you doing, Mel?” Monica asked, as she always did, not expecting a response.

Nodding slowly, I hugged her long and hard, then looked into her eyes and said the first words I’d uttered since I’d been incarcerated, “Better than yesterday, not as well as tomorrow.”

“That’s good,” she replied. “You’re getting better.” She didn’t ask me to say anything more. My sister is an angel who walks on earth.

We strolled to the corner of the lounge, where two overstuffed chairs faced one of the windows that overlooked the courtyard. Monica began her weekly synopsis of life back home. I listened to her discourse as I watched the squirrels outside. She told me that Anita asked about me and was hoping to be able to visit soon. She was doing well in school and had tried out for the football cheerleading squad. Anita and Frank used to spend football season glued to the television set. Each had their own fantasy team, and they loved the competition.

Monica talked about home and told me that my daughter missed me. She said that it wouldn't be long before Anita could accompany her on a visit. I wasn't sure if I wanted Anita to see me here or not.

We heard the rattle and squeak of Linda's drink cart as she moved from table to table, offering drinks to the residents and guests at Mayville. When Linda got to our table, Monica said, "Melanie told me she's doing better today."

"That's certainly good news," Linda said with a wide grin. "Would you like some ginger ale to celebrate?"

Though Linda had directed her question toward Monica, I answered, "Yes. Thank you."

Scooping ice into two cups, she filled them with ginger ale and set them on the table. She reached for my hand, gave it a quick squeeze, and said, "You're welcome. If you need anything else, just give me a holler."

Still smiling, Linda moved to the next table. I had spoken twice today and was crawling back to my family and whatever life I could rebuild. I picked up my ginger ale and tipped the cup toward my sister, as if offering a toast. She reached for her cup, touched its edge to mine and smiling, we sipped the drinks.

"I've missed you so much," Monica told me.

"I've missed you, too." I responded, ready to tell her what had happened the night Frank died.

Before I had a chance to begin, we heard a crashing noise, followed by a shriek. Turning toward the sound, I saw Linda lying on the floor. Her cart was overturned. Felicia, a longtime resident, was swinging a chair and moving toward my sister. Monica was motionless, unable to turn her eyes away from Felicia.

Without hesitating, I stepped between my sister and the furniture wielding attacker. Felicia swung the wooden chair with all her strength, connecting with my right temple. I dropped like a rock as the blood flowed from my head. I know this because I watched the gruesome scene as I hovered above the commotion.

Janet had been in the far corner of the lounge. She got to Felicia before she could strike another blow. Somehow wresting the chair from the young patient, Janet hustled Felicia to the infirmary, where a nurse took charge of the situation and sedated the agitated woman.

Monica was on her knees, bending over me and murmuring encouragement. She didn't know that I was no longer in my body. I called out to Monica. I wanted to tell her I wasn't really gone, but she couldn't hear me.

I felt a hand on my shoulder and turned to see Frank standing by my side.

"Oh, Frank, I'm so sorry for what I did, forever thinking you'd do anything to harm Anita."

My husband took my hand in his. Sadly, he shook his head and whispered, "I love you and I love our daughter. I know you do, too. Sometimes love has unintended consequences."

###

Thank you for reading Long Stories Short. Please take a minute to post a rating or a review. It would be helpful and much appreciated.

Amazon.com: Long Stories Short: A collection of short stories by eBook : Black, Karen: Kindle Store

About the Author

Writing in a variety of genres, Black combines imagination and experience to weave plots with memorable characters in descriptive settings, whether contemporary or supernatural.

Author of four novels and a dozen novelettes and short stories, her fascination with the paranormal is often seen in her prose, as is her passion for animals. Even when it isn't the basis of the plot, the author typically includes a four-legged character in her storyline, even if just a cameo appearance. Her website, www.storiesbykaren.org details her publications.

Black lives in the United States with her husband, and two alien creatures disguised as cats. One of them is rumored to be ET's second cousin. The rumor, however, has not been confirmed.

***

Turn the page for a preview of ***A Wish and His Demand***.

When her childhood wish comes true, Amanda becomes a successful author. But later, she is faced with a cost that is more than she is willing to pay. With help from a longtime friend and a telepathic cat, she learns that love has many forms.

A Wish and His Demand

Chapter One

Amanda squinted and pointed toward the sky. "Look, Momma. There's a giant cat!"

Marjorie followed her daughter's gaze. Fluffy cumulus clouds blended with wispy cirrus and formed the image of a huge cat.

"It's a white lion, and she looks like Jonah's cat, Vanilla. She sleeps in the clouds all day and prowls the backyard at night to protect us from anything bad. White lions are magical and invisible. Vanilla, the lion, can grant wishes and tell the future."

"The way you and Jonah come up with stories, you two should write a book someday," Marjorie chuckled. Jonah's and Amanda's families lived on the same block. The children had been friends since kindergarten.

"Yep. Jonah and I are going to be famous authors."

The pair watched the giant cat until she disappeared. Amanda reached for her mother's hand, and they strolled through the maze of tables at the County Fairgrounds. The Fairgrounds had been used as a weekend flea market since Marjorie was a youngster, and buyers came from miles around. As Marjorie scanned the antiques, Amanda spotted an old woman sitting alone. She dropped her mother's hand.

"I'm going over there," she said, pointing in the direction where the old lady sat.

"Okay, don't wander any farther."

Amanda skipped across the pathway to a small stand at the edge of the market and began an animated conversation with the woman.

"Look at this!" Amanda held up an ink pen when her mother joined her. Made from silver, with a lustrous cat etched on the barrel, the tarnished antique had a dent on the side. The feline looked ready to pounce and when the sunlight hit the pen, the cat's eyes flashed, like fire was shooting from them.

"I'll bet this pen could write books full of stories," Amanda said.

The old-fashioned writing tip was in perfect condition, and while Marjorie wondered at the wisdom of trusting Amanda with a bottle of ink, she was charmed by her daughter's captivation with the instrument.

"A little polish and this pen will sparkle," Marjorie said. "We can stop at the bookshop and find some ink."

"How much for the pen?" Marjorie asked the woman.

Grey, wispy hair was pulled back from the woman's forehead and wound around her head in an old-fashioned braid. Her eyes sparkled like those of a youngster. The woman took the pen from Marjorie, lifted it to her lips and blew a gentle breath across it. "So much dust today."

She turned her attention to Amanda. "This pen is a gift. It will help you write wonderful stories. You'll need ink, too." The woman reached under the table and produced a one-inch square bottle filled with ink and closed with a crystal stopper.

"That is so kind of you. Can I at least pay you for the ink?" Marjorie asked.

"No, no, no. A pen isn't any good without ink."

"Thank you very much," Amanda said with a wide grin.

"You are welcome. If you take care of the pen, it will take care of you," the old woman said with a wink and a smile.

A slight breeze encircled the table and stirred up the dust like a mini tornado. Marjorie shivered. Fascinated by the pen, Amanda was oblivious to the wind. As she watched the tarnish slowly fade from the silver, the dent in the pen's barrel also disappeared. She was about to show her mother when Marjorie's phone buzzed.

"Is this Marjorie Winston?" an unfamiliar voice asked.

"Yes."

"I'm calling from the Metro Police Department. Your husband was involved in an accident and has been taken to Metro Community Hospital."

"What happened?" Marjorie gasped.

"I don't have the details, but a doctor will meet you in the Emergency Room."

"I'll be there in ten minutes."

"What's wrong, Momma?"

"Daddy got hurt in a car wreck."

"Is he okay?"

"I hope so," Marjorie replied.

Amanda patted her mother's knee before a slight rumble from her pen distracted her. It vibrated like Vanilla when she purred.

At the hospital, Marjorie grabbed Amanda's hand and rushed to the ER. "I'm here to see James Winston!"

"You can have a seat by the door," the nurse told her. "I'll tell the doctor you're here."

Marjorie directed Amanda to a chair, then paced the floor while she waited. It seemed like an hour, but within a few minutes, a doctor walked into the room.

"Mrs. Winston?"

"Yes! Can I see my husband, please?"

"Come with me."

Amanda rushed to her mother's side, and they followed the doctor through the double doors, down the hall, and into a small waiting room filled with the aroma of fresh coffee. The doctor turned to Amanda.

"Would you mind waiting here for a couple of minutes while I talk to your mom?"

"Okay," Amanda said.

With a sense of dread, Marjorie followed the doctor into a small cubicle, where her husband lay with an array of wires and tubes attached to his arms and chest. Layers of gauze encircled his head like an oversized turban. His usually rose-colored cheeks were colorless.

Although she knew the answer, Marjorie asked, "How bad is it?"

"It is a miracle that he has survived this long. A tractor-trailer hit a pillar directly above him. Concrete fell and crushed the car. The machines are keeping him alive but won't help for much longer. The damage to his brain is irreversible and the internal injuries are irreparable."

Marjorie's knees buckled. With the doctor's support, she approached her husband's bed.

"I'll leave you alone."

With trembling fingers, Marjorie covered his hand. "If not for Amanda, I would join you tonight."

After Amanda's father died, her mother barely functioned. Although he left a substantial life insurance policy to provide for them, Marjorie got a part-time job and did her best to hide the depression that consumed her.

Amanda grew up faster than she would otherwise have done. She missed her dad, worried about her mom, and gradually took over the household chores. During the day, she concentrated on her schoolwork. Every evening, she got lost in writing with her beautiful silver pen and became increasingly reclusive.

Partially because of the added responsibility and the emotional support that she provided for her mother, the larger reason for Amanda's solitude was her lack of interest in any social activities. Except for her relationship with Jonah, her only interest was writing.

"Amanda, you won't believe this!" Jonah said, bursting

into her kitchen, wrapping his arms around her, and lifting her off the floor.

"Won't believe what?" She laughed as she hugged him, thrilled to see him so excited.

"I've been accepted at Kings College in London! Their program in English and Linguistics is one of the top ten in the world! And I'm going to intern at the Cambridge Publishing House!"

Amanda's excitement turned to apprehension. "London? London, England?"

"Of course, London, England, silly. I'm leaving in three weeks. Come with me, Manda. We'll stay with my aunt and uncle. They would welcome you. I've already asked. And I have enough money saved to pay for your trip. I'll take care of you, and we'll write dozens of books like we've always planned."

"You know my mother will never leave this house and I can't abandon her."

"It won't be so different from you leaving for college next year," he said.

"I'm planning to apply to Wyatt University, so that I can commute from home."

"Nothing will be the same without you. Don't say no. Just think about it."

"I'll think about it." They both knew that their time together was about to end.

During their first few years apart, they stayed in touch. Jonah graduated, and the publishing company offered him a permanent position. His new career, and the distance between them, made it increasingly difficult to keep in close contact, and he still couldn't convince Amanda to join him in London.

On the tenth anniversary of her father's death, Amanda got a phone call.

"Good afternoon, Ms. Winston. This is Metro General Hospital. Can you come to the hospital? Your mother has been involved in an accident."

As she disconnected the call, Amanda knew that her mother had gone to join her dad. When she got to the hospital, they told her that her mother had lost control of her car and hit a concrete pillar. It happened on the overpass directly above the spot where Amanda's father had crashed ten years prior. Whether it was an uncanny coincidence or an orchestrated ending to her mother's life, Amanda took comfort in the belief that her parents were together again.

Chapter Two

Ten years later

The year after her mother passed away, Amanda bought a small farm a few miles from where she had grown up. Close enough to town to allow for convenient shopping, the house was far enough away to ensure tranquility.

Sprawled in an overstuffed recliner, she balanced a laptop computer on her knees. Her long, graceful fingers moved effortlessly over the keyboard. Perched on the back of the couch, a golden-eyed cat batted at her hair.

"Are you bored, Odin?"

The cat chirped in response.

"I'm almost done. Give me thirty minutes and you can have my full attention."

As if he understood, the ivory-colored cat arched his back Halloween-style, then collapsed into a furry ball, closed his eyes, and settled down to wait.

Finally finished, Amanda glanced at her pen in the silk-lined wooden box where it was cradled. A bottle of ink sat next to the pen. It was the same bottle that the old woman had given her.

Never replenished, it was always full.

Even with the ever-evolving technology, Amanda used her pen to write every word of each novel before she transferred the finished product to the computer. She had tried typing her manuscripts, but writer's block always took over when she stared at the screen. The old silver relic functioned as her muse, and she was fine with that arrangement.

###

A Wish and His Demand is on sale at Amazon.com.
https://amzn.to/3AppHml

Publications

Goldfield Forest
Rustic Acres
A Wish and His Demand
For Eternity
Race into Murder
Ride into Romance
Deadly Repercussions
One Random Act of Violence
Mountain Justice
Vindictive Angel
Close Your Eyes and They're Gone
Elusive Guardians
Life's Highway to Love

***

Connect with the Author

Website: www.storiesbykaren.org

Amazon: http://www.amazon.com/Karen-Black/e/B00B0WCR44

Facebook: https://www.facebook.com/pages/Karen-Black-Author/446827615394900

Made in the USA
Columbia, SC
29 November 2024